Love Among the Chickens

Love Among the Chickens

the Chickens

P.G. Wodehouse

MINT EDITIONS

Love Among the Chickens was first published in 1906.

This edition published by Mint Editions 2021.

ISBN 9781513270777 | E-ISBN 9781513275772

Published by Mint Editions®

 MINT
EDITIONS

minteditionbooks.com

Publishing Director: Jennifer Newens
Design & Production: Rachel Lopez Metzger
Typesetting: Westchester Publishing Services

Contents

I

A Letter With a Postscript

Agentleman called to see you when you were out last night, sir," said Mrs. Medley, my landlady, removing the last of the breakfast things.

"Yes?" I said, in my affable way.

"A gentleman," said Mrs. Medley meditatively, "with a very powerful voice."

"Caruso?"

"Sir?"

"I said, did he leave a name?"

"Yes, sir. Mr. Ukridge."

"Oh, my sainted aunt!"

"Sir!"

"Nothing, nothing."

"Thank you, sir," said Mrs. Medley, withdrawing from the presence.

Ukridge! Oh, hang it! I had not met him for years, and, glad as I am, as a general thing, to see the friends of my youth when they drop in for a chat, I doubted whether I was quite equal to Ukridge at the moment. A stout fellow in both the physical and moral sense of the words, he was a trifle too jumpy for a man of my cloistered and intellectual life, especially as just now I was trying to plan out a new novel, a tricky job demanding complete quiet and seclusion. It had always been my experience that, when Ukridge was around, things began to happen swiftly and violently, rendering meditation impossible. Ukridge was the sort of man who asks you out to dinner, borrows the money from you to pay the bill, and winds up the evening by embroiling you in a fight with a cabman. I have gone to Covent Garden balls with Ukridge, and found myself legging it down Henrietta Street in the grey dawn, pursued by infuriated costermongers.

I wondered how he had got my address, and on that problem light was immediately cast by Mrs. Medley, who returned, bearing an envelope.

"It came by the morning post, sir, but it was left at Number Twenty by mistake."

"Oh, thank you."

"Thank you, sir," said Mrs. Medley.

I recognised the handwriting. The letter, which bore a Devonshire postmark, was from an artist friend of mine, one Lickford, who was at present on a sketching tour in the west. I had seen him off at Waterloo a week before, and I remember that I had walked away from the station wishing that I could summon up the energy to pack and get off to the country somewhere. I hate London in July.

The letter was a long one, but it was the postscript which interested me most.

". . . By the way, at Yeovil I ran into an old friend of ours, Stanley Featherstonehaugh Ukridge, of all people. As large as life—quite six foot two, and tremendously filled out. I thought he was abroad. The last I heard of him was that he had started for Buenos Ayres in a cattle ship, with a borrowed pipe by way of luggage. It seems he has been in England for some time. I met him in the refreshment-room at Yeovil Station. I was waiting for a down train; he had changed on his way to town. As I opened the door, I heard a huge voice entreating the lady behind the bar to 'put it in a pewter'; and there was S. F. U. in a villainous old suit of grey flannels (I'll swear it was the one he had on last time I saw him) with pince-nez tacked on to his ears with ginger-beer wire as usual, and a couple of inches of bare neck showing between the bottom of his collar and the top of his coat—you remember how he could never get a stud to do its work. He also wore a mackintosh, though it was a blazing day.

"He greeted me with effusive shouts. Wouldn't hear of my standing the racket. Insisted on being host. When we had finished, he fumbled in his pockets, looked pained and surprised, and drew me aside. 'Look here, Licky, old horse,' he said, 'you know I never borrow money. It's against my principles. But I *must* have a couple of bob. Can you, my dear good fellow, oblige me with a couple of bob till next Tuesday? I'll tell you what I'll do. (In a voice full of emotion). I'll let you have this (producing a beastly little threepenny bit with a hole in it which he had probably picked up in the street) until I can pay you back. This is of more value to me than I can well express, Licky, my boy. A very, very dear friend gave it to me when we parted, years ago. . . It's a wrench. . . Still,—no, no. . . You must take it, you must take it. Licky, old man, shake hands, old horse. Shake hands, my boy.' He then tottered to the bar, deeply moved, and paid up out of the five shillings which he had made it as an after-thought. He asked after you, and said you were one of the noblest men on earth. I gave him your address, not being able to get out of it, but if I were you I should fly while there is yet time."

IT SEEMED TO ME THAT the advice was good and should be followed. I needed a change of air. London may have suited Doctor Johnson, but in the summer time it is not for the ordinary man. What I wanted, to enable me to give the public of my best (as the reviewer of a weekly paper, dealing with my last work, had expressed a polite hope that I would continue to do) was a little haven in the country somewhere.

I rang the bell.

"Sir?" said Mrs. Medley.

"I'm going away for a bit," I said.

"Yes, sir."

"I don't know where. I'll send you the address, so that you can forward letters."

"Yes, sir."

"And, if Mr. Ukridge calls again. . ."

At this point a thunderous knocking on the front door interrupted me. Something seemed to tell me who was at the end of that knocker. I heard Mrs. Medley's footsteps pass along the hall. There was the click of the latch. A volume of sound rushed up the stairs.

"Is Mr. Garnet in? Where is he? Show me the old horse. Where is the man of wrath? Exhibit the son of Belial."

There followed a violent crashing on the stairs, shaking the house.

"Garnet! Where are you, laddie? Garnet!! GARNET!!!!!"

Stanley Featherstonehaugh Ukridge was in my midst.

II

Mr. and Mrs. S. F. Ukridge

I have often thought that Who's Who, though a bulky and well-meaning volume, omits too many of England's greatest men. It is not comprehensive enough. I am in it, nestling among the G's:—

"Garnet, Jeremy, o.s. of late Henry Garnet, vicar of Much Middlefold, Salop; author. Publications: 'The Outsider,' 'The Manoeuvres of Arthur.' Hobbies: Cricket, football, swimming, golf. Clubs: Arts."

But if you search among the U's for UKRIDGE, Stanley Featherstonehaugh, details of whose tempestuous career would make really interesting reading, you find no mention of him. It seems unfair, though I imagine Ukridge bears it with fortitude. That much-enduring man has had a lifetime's training in bearing things with fortitude.

He seemed in his customary jovial spirits now, as he dashed into the room, clinging on to the pince-nez which even ginger-beer wire rarely kept stable for two minutes together.

"My dear old man," he shouted, springing at me and seizing my hand in the grip like the bite of a horse. "How *are* you, old buck? This is good. By Jove, this is fine, what?"

He dashed to the door and looked out.

"Come on Millie! Pick up the waukeesis. Here's old Garnet, looking just the same as ever. Devilish handsome fellow! You'll be glad you came when you see him. Beats the Zoo hollow!"

There appeared round the corner of Ukridge a young woman. She paused in the doorway and smiled pleasantly.

"Garny, old horse," said Ukridge with some pride, "this is *her*! The pride of the home. Companion of joys and sorrows and all the rest of it. In fact," in a burst of confidence, "my wife."

I bowed awkwardly. The idea of Ukridge married was something too overpowering to be readily assimilated.

"Buck up, old horse," said Ukridge encouragingly. He had a painful habit of addressing all and sundry by that title. In his school-master days—at one period of his vivid career he and I had been colleagues on the staff of a private school—he had made use of it interviewing the parents of new pupils, and the latter had gone away, as a rule, with a feeling that this must be either the easy manner of Genius or due to alcohol, and hoping for the best. He also used it to perfect strangers in the streets, and on one occasion had been heard to address a bishop by that title, rendering that dignitary, as Mr. Baboo Jaberjee would put it, *sotto voce* with gratification. "Surprised to find me married, what? Garny, old boy,"—sinking his voice to a whisper almost inaudible on the other side of the street—"take my tip. Go and jump off the dock yourself. You'll feel another man. Give up this bachelor business. It's a mug's game. I look on you bachelors as excrescences on the social system. I regard you, old man, purely and simply as a wart. Go and get married, laddie, go and get married. By gad, I've forgotten to pay the cabby. Lend me a couple of bob, Garny old chap."

He was out of the door and on his way downstairs before the echoes of his last remark had ceased to shake the window. I was left to entertain Mrs. Ukridge.

So far her share in the conversation had been confined to the pleasant smile which was apparently her chief form of expression. Nobody talked very much when Ukridge was present. She sat on the edge of the armchair, looking very small and quiet. I was conscious of feeling a benevolent pity for her. If I had been a girl, I would have preferred to marry a volcano. A little of Ukridge, as his former head master had once said in a moody, reflective voice, went a very long way. "You and Stanley have known each other a long time, haven't you?" said the object of my commiseration, breaking the silence.

"Yes. Oh, yes. Several years. We were masters at the same school."

Mrs. Ukridge leaned forward with round, shining eyes.

"Really? Oh, how nice!" she said ecstatically.

Not yet, to judge from her expression and the tone of her voice, had she found any disadvantages attached to the arduous position of being Mrs. Stanley Ukridge.

"He's a wonderfully versatile man," I said.

"I believe he could do anything."

"He'd have a jolly good try!"

"Have you ever kept fowls?" asked Mrs. Ukridge, with apparent irrelevance.

I had not. She looked disappointed.

"I was hoping you might have had some experience. Stanley, of course, can turn his hand to anything; but I think experience is rather a good thing, don't you?"

"Yes. But. . ."

"I have bought a shilling book called 'Fowls and All About Them,' and this week's copy of C.A.C."

"C.A.C.?"

"*Chiefly About Chickens*. It's a paper, you know. But it's all rather hard to understand. You see, we. . . but here is Stanley. He will explain the whole thing."

"Well, Garny, old horse," said Ukridge, re-entering the room after another energetic passage of the stairs. "Years since I saw you. Still buzzing along?"

"Still, so to speak, buzzing," I assented.

"I was reading your last book the other day."

"Yes?" I said, gratified. "How did you like it?"

"Well, as a matter of fact, laddie, I didn't get beyond the third page, because the scurvy knave at the bookstall said he wasn't running a free library, and in one way and another there was a certain amount of unpleasantness. Still, it seemed bright and interesting up to page three. But let's settle down and talk business. I've got a scheme for you, Garny old man. Yessir, the idea of a thousand years. Now listen to me for a moment. Let me get a word in edgeways."

He sat down on the table, and dragged up a chair as a leg-rest. Then he took off his pince-nez, wiped them, re-adjusted the ginger-beer wire behind his ears, and, having hit a brown patch on the knee of his grey flannel trousers several times, in the apparent hope of removing it, resumed:

"About fowls."

The subject was beginning to interest me. It showed a curious tendency to creep into the conversation of the Ukridge family.

"I want you to give me your undivided attention for a moment. I was saying to my wife, as we came here, 'Garnet's the man! Clever devil, Garnet. Full of ideas.' Didn't I, Millie?"

"Yes, dear."

"Laddie," said Ukridge impressively, "we are going to keep fowls."

He shifted himself farther on to the table and upset the ink-pot.

"Never mind," he said, "it'll soak in. It's good for the texture. Or am I thinking of tobacco-ash on the carpet? Well, never mind. Listen to me! When I said that we were going to keep fowls, I didn't mean in a small, piffling sort of way—two cocks and a couple of hens and a golf-ball for a nest-egg. We are going to do it on a large scale. We are going to run a chicken farm!"

"A chicken farm," echoed Mrs. Ukridge with an affectionate and admiring glance at her husband.

"Ah," I said, feeling my responsibilities as chorus. "A chicken farm."

"I've thought it all over, laddie, and it's as clear as mud. No expenses, large profits, quick returns. Chickens, eggs, and the money streaming in faster than you can bank it. Winter and summer underclothing, my bonny boy, lined with crackling Bradbury's. It's the idea of a lifetime. Now listen to me for a moment. You get your hen—"

"One hen?"

"Call it one for the sake of argument. It makes my calculations clearer. Very well, then. Harriet the hen—you get her. Do you follow me so far?"

"Yes. You get a hen."

"I told you Garnet was a dashed bright fellow," said Ukridge approvingly to his attentive wife. "Notice the way he keeps right after one's ideas? Like a bloodhound. Well, where was I?"

"You'd just got a hen."

"Exactly. The hen. Pricilla the pullet. Well, it lays an egg every day of the week. You sell the eggs, six for half a crown. Keep of hen costs nothing. Profit—at least a couple of bob on every dozen eggs. What do you think of that?"

"I think I'd like to overhaul the figures in case of error."

"Error!" shouted Ukridge, pounding the table till it groaned. "Error? Not a bit of it. Can't you follow a simple calculation like that? Oh, I forgot to say that you get—and here is the nub of the thing—you get your first hen on tick. Anybody will be glad to let you have the hen on tick. Well, then, you let this hen—this first, original hen, this on-tick-hen—you let it set and hatch chickens. Now follow me closely. Suppose you have a dozen hens. Very well, then. When each of the dozen has a dozen chickens, you send the old hens back to the chappies you borrowed them from, with thanks for kind loan; and there you are, starting business with a hundred and forty-four free chickens to your name. And after a bit, when the chickens grow up and begin to lay, all you have to do is to sit back in your chair and endorse the big cheques. Isn't that so, Millie?"

"Yes, dear."

"We've fixed it all up. Do you know Combe Regis, in Dorsetshire? On the borders of Devon. Bathing. Sea-air. Splendid scenery. Just the place for a chicken farm. A friend of Millie's—girl she knew at school— has lent us a topping old house, with large grounds. All we've got to do is to get in the fowls. I've ordered the first lot. We shall find them waiting for us when we arrive."

"Well," I said, "I'm sure I wish you luck. Mind you let me know how you get on."

"Let you know!" roared Ukridge. "Why, my dear old horse, you're coming with us."

"Am I?" I said blankly.

"Certainly you are. We shall take no refusal. Will we, Millie?"

"No, dear."

"Of course not. No refusal of any sort. Pack up tonight and meet us at Waterloo tomorrow."

"It's awfully good of you. . ."

"Not a bit of it—not a bit of it. This is pure business. I was saying to Millie as we came along that you were the very man for us. A man with your flow of ideas will be invaluable on a chicken farm. Absolutely invaluable. You see," proceeded Ukridge, "I'm one of those practical fellows. The hard-headed type. I go straight ahead, following my nose. What you want in a business of this sort is a touch of the dreamer to help out the practical mind. We look to you for suggestions, laddie. Flashes of inspiration and all that sort of thing. Of course, you take your share of the profits. That's understood. Yes, yes, I must insist. Strict business between friends. Now, taking it that, at a conservative estimate, the net profits for the first fiscal year amount to—five thousand, no, better be on the safe side—say, four thousand five hundred pounds. . . But we'll arrange all that end of it when we get down there. Millie will look after that. She's the secretary of the concern. She's been writing letters to people asking for hens. So you see it's a thoroughly organised business. How many hen-letters did you write last week, old girl?"

"Ten, dear."

Ukridge turned triumphantly to me.

"You hear? Ten. Ten letters asking for hens. That's the way to succeed. Push and enterprise."

"Six of them haven't answered, Stanley, dear, and the rest refused."

"Immaterial," said Ukridge with a grand gesture. "That doesn't matter. The point is that the letters were written. It shows we are solid and practical. Well now, can you get your things ready by tomorrow, Garny old horse?"

Strange how one reaches an epoch-making moment in one's life without recognising it. If I had refused that invitation, I would not have—at any rate, I would have missed a remarkable experience. It is not given to everyone to see Stanley Featherstonehaugh Ukridge manage a chicken farm.

"I was thinking of going somewhere where I could get some golf," I said undecidedly.

"Combe Regis is just the place for you, then. Perfect hot-bed of golf. Full of the finest players. Can't throw a brick without hitting an amateur champion. Grand links at the top of the hill not half a mile from the farm. Bring your clubs. You'll be able to play in the afternoons. Get through serious work by lunch time."

"You know," I said, "I am absolutely inexperienced as regards fowls. I just know enough to help myself to bread sauce when I see one, but no more."

"Excellent! You're just the man. You will bring to the work a mind unclouded by theories. You will act solely by the light of your intelligence. And you've got lots of that. That novel of yours showed the most extraordinary intelligence—at least as far as that blighter at the bookstall would let me read. I wouldn't have a professional chicken farmer about the place if he paid to come. If he applied to me, I should simply send him away. Natural intelligence is what we want. Then we can rely on you?"

"Very well," I said slowly. "It's very kind of you to ask me."

"Business, laddie, pure business. Very well, then. We shall catch the eleven-twenty at Waterloo. Don't miss it. Look out for me on the platform. If I see you first, I'll shout."

III

Waterloo Station, Some Fellow-Travellers, and a Girl With Brown Hair

The austerity of Waterloo Station was lightened on the following morning at ten minutes to eleven, when I arrived to catch the train to Combe Regis, by several gleams of sunshine and a great deal of bustle and activity on the various platforms. A porter took my suitcase and golf-clubs, and arranged an assignation on Number 6 platform. I bought my ticket, and made my way to the bookstall, where, in the interests of trade, I inquired in a loud and penetrating voice if they had got Jeremy Garnet's "Manoeuvres of Arthur." Being informed that they had not, I clicked my tongue reproachfully, advised them to order in a supply, as the demand was likely to be large, and spent a couple of shillings on a magazine and some weekly papers. Then, with ten minutes to spare, I went off in search of Ukridge.

I found him on platform six. The eleven-twenty was already alongside, and presently I observed my porter cleaving a path towards me with the suit-case and golf-bag.

"Here you are!" shouted Ukridge vigorously. "Good for you. Thought you were going to miss it."

I shook hands with the smiling Mrs. Ukridge.

"I've got a carriage and collared two corner seats. Millie goes down in another. She doesn't like the smell of smoke when she's travelling. Hope we get the carriage to ourselves. Devil of a lot of people here this morning. Still, the more people there are in the world, the more eggs we shall sell. I can see with half an eye that all these blighters are confirmed egg-eaters. Get in, sonnie. I'll just see the missis into her carriage, and come back to you."

I entered the compartment, and stood at the door, looking out in the faint hope of thwarting an invasion of fellow-travellers. Then I withdrew my head suddenly and sat down. An elderly gentleman, accompanied by a pretty girl, was coming towards me. It was not this type of fellow traveller whom I had hoped to keep out. I had noticed the girl at the booking office. She had waited by the side of the queue while the elderly gentleman struggled gamely for the tickets, and I had had plenty of opportunity of observing her appearance. I had debated with myself whether her hair should rightly be described as brown or golden. I had finally decided on brown. Once only had I met her eyes, and then only for an instant. They might be blue. They might be grey. I could not be certain. Life is full of these problems.

"This seems to be tolerably empty, my dear Phyllis," said the elderly gentleman, coming to the door of the compartment and looking in. "You're sure you don't object to a smoking-carriage?"

"Oh no, father. Not a bit."

"Then I think. . ." said the elderly gentleman, getting in.

The inflection of his voice suggested the Irishman. It was not a brogue. There were no strange words. But the general effect was Irish.

"That's good," he said, settling himself and pulling out a cigar case.

The bustle of the platform had increased momentarily, until now, when, from the snorting of the engine, it seemed likely that the train might start at any minute, the crowd's excitement was extreme. Shrill cries echoed down the platform. Lost sheep, singly and in companies, rushed to and fro, peering eagerly into carriages in search of seats. Piercing voices ordered unknown "Tommies" and "Ernies" to "keep by aunty, now." Just as Ukridge returned, that *sauve qui peut* of the railway crowd, the dreaded "Get in anywhere," began to be heard, and the next moment an avalanche of warm humanity poured into the carriage.

The newcomers consisted of a middle-aged lady, addressed as Aunty, very stout and clad in a grey alpaca dress, skin-tight; a youth called Albert, not, it was to appear, a sunny child; a niece of some twenty years, stolid and seemingly without interest in life, and one or two other camp-followers and retainers.

Ukridge slipped into his corner, adroitly foiling Albert, who had made a dive in that direction. Albert regarded him fixedly and reproachfully for a space, then sank into the seat beside me and began to chew something that smelt of aniseed.

Aunty, meanwhile, was distributing her substantial weight evenly between the feet of the Irish gentleman and those of his daughter, as she leaned out of the window to converse with a lady friend in a straw hat and hair curlers, accompanied by three dirty and frivolous boys. It was, she stated, lucky that she had caught the train. I could not agree with her. The girl with the brown hair and the eyes that were neither blue or grey was bearing the infliction, I noticed, with angelic calm. She even smiled. This was when the train suddenly moved off with a jerk, and Aunty, staggering back, sat down on the bag of food which Albert had placed on the seat beside him.

"Clumsy!" observed Albert tersely.

"*Albert*, you mustn't speak to Aunty so!"

"Wodyer want to sit on my bag for then?" said Albert disagreeably.

They argued the point. Argument in no wise interfered with Albert's power of mastication. The odour of aniseed became more and more painful. Ukridge had lighted a cigar, and I understood why Mrs. Ukridge preferred to travel in another compartment, for

> *"In his hand he bore the brand*
> *Which none but he might smoke."*

I looked across the carriage stealthily to see how the girl was enduring this combination of evils, and noticed that she had begun to read. And as she put the book down to look out of the window, I saw with a thrill that trickled like warm water down my spine that her book was "The Manoeuvres of Arthur." I gasped. That a girl should look as pretty as that and at the same time have the rare intelligence to read Me. . . well, it seemed an almost superhuman combination of the excellencies. And more devoutly than ever I cursed in my heart these intrusive outsiders who had charged in at the last moment and destroyed for ever my chance of making this wonderful girl's acquaintance. But for them, we might have become intimate in the first half hour. As it was, what were we? Ships that pass in the night! She would get out at some beastly wayside station, and vanish from my life without my ever having even spoken to her.

Aunty, meanwhile, having retired badly worsted from her encounter with Albert, who showed a skill in logomachy that marked him out as a future labour member, was consoling herself with meat sandwiches. The niece was demolishing sausage rolls. The atmosphere of the carriage was charged with a blend of odours, topping all Ukridge's cigar, now in full blast.

The train raced on towards the sea. It was a warm day, and a torpid peace began to settle down upon the carriage. Ukridge had thrown away the stump of his cigar, and was now leaning back with his mouth open and his eyes shut. Aunty, still clutching a much-bitten section of a beef sandwich, was breathing heavily and swaying from side to side.

P.G. WODEHOUSE

Albert and the niece were dozing, Albert's jaws working automatically, even in sleep.

"What's your book, my dear?" asked the Irishman.

"'The Manoeuvres of Arthur,' father. By Jeremy Garnet."

I would not have believed without the evidence of my ears that my name could possibly have sounded so musical.

"Molly McEachern gave it to me when I left the Abbey. She keeps a shelf of books for her guests when they are going away. Books that she considers rubbish, and doesn't want, you know."

I hated Miss McEachern without further evidence.

"And what do you think of it?"

"I like it," said the girl decidedly. The carriage swam before my eyes. "I think it is very clever."

What did it matter after that that the ass in charge of the Waterloo bookstall had never heard of "The Manoeuvres of Arthur," and that my publishers, whenever I slunk in to ask how it was selling, looked at me with a sort of grave, paternal pity and said that it had not really "begun to move?" Anybody can write one of those rotten popular novels which appeal to the unthinking public, but it takes a man of intellect and refinement and taste and all that sort of thing to turn out something that will be approved of by a girl like this.

"I wonder who Jeremy Garnet is," she said. "I've never heard of him before. I imagine him rather an old young man, probably with an eyeglass, and conceited. And I should think he didn't know many girls. At least if he thinks Pamela an ordinary sort of girl. She's a cr-r-eature," said Phyllis emphatically.

This was a blow to me. I had always looked on Pamela as a well-drawn character, and a very attractive, kittenish little thing at that. That scene between her and the curate in the conservatory. . . And when she talks to Arthur at the meet of the Blankshires. . . I was sorry she did not like Pamela. Somehow it lowered Pamela in my estimation.

"But I like Arthur," said the girl.

This was better. A good chap, Arthur,—a very complete and thoughtful study of myself. If she liked Arthur, why, then it followed. . . but what was the use? I should never get a chance of speaking to her. We were divided by a great gulf of Aunties and Alberts and meat sandwiches.

The train was beginning to slow down. Signs of returning animation began to be noticeable among the sleepers. Aunty's eyes opened, stared vacantly round, closed, and reopened. The niece woke, and started instantly to attack a sausage roll. Albert and Ukridge slumbered on.

A whistle from the engine, and the train drew up at a station. Looking out, I saw that it was Yeovil. There was a general exodus. Aunty became instantly a thing of dash and electricity, collected parcels, shook Albert, replied to his thrusts with repartee, and finally heading a stampede out of the door.

The Irishman and his daughter also rose, and got out. I watched them leave stoically. It would have been too much to expect that they should be going any further.

"Where are we?" said Ukridge sleepily. "Yeovil? Not far now. I tell you what it is, old horse, I could do with a drink."

With that remark he closed his eyes again, and returned to his slumbers. And, as he did so, my eye, roving discontentedly over the carriage, was caught by something lying in the far corner. It was "The Manoeuvres of Arthur." The girl had left it behind.

I suppose what follows shows the vanity that obsesses young authors. It did not even present itself to me as a tenable theory that the book might have been left behind on purpose, as being of no further use to the owner. It only occurred to me that, if I did not act swiftly, the poor girl would suffer a loss beside which the loss of a purse or vanity-case were trivial.

Five seconds later I was on the platform.

"Excuse me," I said, "I think. . . ?"

"Oh, thank you so much," said the girl.

I made my way back to the carriage, and lit my pipe in a glow of emotion.

"They are blue," I said to my immortal soul. "A wonderful, deep, soft, heavenly blue, like the sea at noonday."

IV

The Arrival

From Axminster to Combe Regis the line runs through country as attractive as any that can be found in the island, and the train, as if in appreciation of this fact, does not hurry over the journey. It was late afternoon by the time we reached our destination.

The arrangements for the carrying of luggage at Combe Regis border on the primitive. Boxes are left on the platform, and later, when he thinks of it, a carrier looks in and conveys them into the valley and up the hill on the opposite side to the address written on the labels. The owner walks. Combe Regis is not a place for the halt and maimed.

Ukridge led us in the direction of the farm, which lay across the valley, looking through woods to the sea. The place was visible from the station, from which, indeed, standing as it did on the top of a hill, the view was extensive.

Half-way up the slope on the other side of the valley we left the road and made our way across a spongy field, Ukridge explaining that this was a short cut. We climbed through a hedge, crossed a stream and another field, and after negotiating a difficult bank, topped with barbed wire, found ourselves in a garden.

Ukridge mopped his forehead, and restored his pince-nez to their original position from which the passage of the barbed wire had dislodged them.

"This is the place," he said. "We've come in by the back way. Saves time. Tired, Millie?"

"A little, dear. I should like some tea."

"Same here," I agreed.

"That'll be all right," said Ukridge. "A most competent man of the name of Beale and his wife are in charge at present. I wrote to them telling them that we were coming today. They will be ready for us. That's the way to do things, Garny old horse. Quiet efficiency. Perfect organisation."

We were at the front door by this time. Ukridge rang the bell. The noise echoed through the house, but there was no answering footsteps. He rang again. There is no mistaking the note of a bell in an empty house. It was plain that the competent man and his wife were out.

"Now what?" I said.

Mrs. Ukridge looked at her husband with calm confidence.

"This," said Ukridge, leaning against the door and endeavouring to button his collar at the back, "reminds me of an afternoon in the Argentine. Two other cheery sportsmen and myself tried for three-quarters of an hour to get into an empty house where there looked as if there might be something to drink, and we'd just got the door open when the owner turned up from behind a tree with a shot-gun. It was a little difficult to explain. As a matter of fact, we never did what you might call really thresh the matter out thoroughly in all its aspects, and you'd be surprised what a devil of a time it takes to pick buck-shot out of a fellow. There was a dog, too."

He broke off, musing dreamily on the happy past, and at this moment history partially repeated itself. From the other side of the door came a dissatisfied whine, followed by a short bark.

"Hullo," said Ukridge, "Beale has a dog." He frowned, annoyed. "What right," he added in an aggrieved tone, "has a beastly mongrel, belonging to a man I employ, to keep me out of my own house? It's a little hard. Here am I, slaving day and night to support Beale, and when I try to get into my own house his infernal dog barks at me. Upon my Sam it's hard!" He brooded for a moment on the injustice of things. "Here, let me get to the keyhole. I'll reason with the brute."

He put his mouth to the keyhole and roared "Goo' dog!" through it. Instantly the door shook as some heavy object hurled itself against it. The barking rang through the house.

"Come round to the back," said Ukridge, giving up the idea of conciliation, "we'll get in through the kitchen window."

The kitchen window proved to be insecurely latched. Ukridge threw it open and we climbed in. The dog, hearing the noise, raced back along the passage and flung himself at the door, scratching at the panels. Ukridge listened with growing indignation.

"Millie, you know how to light a fire. Garnet and I will be collecting cups and things. When that scoundrel Beale arrives I shall tear him limb from limb. Deserting us like this! The man must be a thorough fraud. He told me he was an old soldier. If that's the sort of discipline they used to keep in his regiment, thank God, we've got a Navy! Damn, I've broken a plate. How's the fire getting on, Millie? I'll chop Beale into little bits. What's that you've got there, Garny old horse? Tea? Good. Where's the bread? There goes another plate. Where's Mrs. Beale, too?

By Jove, that woman wants killing as much as her blackguard of a husband. Whoever heard of a cook deliberately leaving her post on the day when her master and mistress were expected back? The abandoned woman. Look here, I'll give that dog three minutes, and if it doesn't stop scratching that door by then, I'll take a rolling pin and go out and have a heart-to-heart talk with it. It's a little hard. My own house, and the first thing I find when I arrive is somebody else's beastly dog scratching holes in the doors and ruining the expensive paint. Stop it, you brute!"

The dog's reply was to continue his operations with immense vigour.

Ukridge's eyes gleamed behind their glasses.

"Give me a good large jug, laddie," he said with ominous calm.

He took the largest of the jugs from the dresser and strode with it into the scullery, whence came a sound of running water. He returned carrying the jug with both hands, his mien that of a general who sees his way to a masterstroke of strategy.

"Garny, old horse," he said, "freeze onto the handle of the door, and, when I give the word, fling wide the gates. Then watch that animal get the surprise of a lifetime."

I attached myself to the handle as directed. Ukridge gave the word. We had a momentary vision of an excited dog of the mongrel class framed in the open doorway, all eyes and teeth; then the passage was occupied by a spreading pool, and indignant barks from the distance told that the enemy was thinking the thing over in some safe retreat.

"Settled *his* hash," said Ukridge complacently. "Nothing like resource, Garny my boy. Some men would have gone on letting a good door be ruined."

"And spoiled the dog for a ha'porth of water," I said.

At this moment Mrs. Ukridge announced that the kettle was boiling. Over a cup of tea Ukridge became the man of business.

"I wonder when those fowls are going to arrive. They should have been here today. It's a little hard. Here am I, all eagerness and anxiety, waiting to start an up-to-date chicken farm, and no fowls! I can't run a chicken farm without fowls. If they don't come tomorrow, I shall get after those people with a hatchet. There must be no slackness. They must bustle about. After tea I'll show you the garden, and we'll choose a place for a fowl-run. Tomorrow we must buckle to. Serious work will begin immediately after breakfast."

"Suppose," I said, "the fowls arrive before we're ready for them?"

"Why, then they must wait."

"But you can't keep fowls cooped up indefinitely in a crate."

"Oh, that'll be all right. There's a basement to this house. We'll let 'em run about there till we're ready for them. There's always a way of doing things if you look for it. Organisation, my boy. That's the watchword. Quiet efficiency."

"I hope you are going to let the hens hatch some of the eggs, dear," said Mrs. Ukridge. "I should love to have some little chickens."

"Of course. By all means. My idea," said Ukridge, "was this. These people will send us fifty fowls of sorts. That means—call it forty-five eggs a day. Let 'em. . . Well, I'm hanged! There's that dog again. Where's the jug?"

But this time an unforeseen interruption prevented the manoeuvre being the success it had been before. I had turned the handle and was about to pull the door open, while Ukridge, looking like some modern and dilapidated version of the *Discobolus*, stood beside me with his jug poised, when a voice spoke from the window.

"Stand still!" said the voice, "or I'll corpse you!"

I dropped the handle. Ukridge dropped the jug. Mrs. Ukridge dropped her tea-cup. At the window, with a double-barrelled gun in his hands, stood a short, square, red-headed man. The muzzle of his gun, which rested on the sill, was pointing in a straight line at the third button of my waistcoat.

Ukridge emitted a roar like that of a hungry lion.

"Beale! You scoundrelly, unprincipled, demon! What the devil are you doing with that gun? Why were you out? What have you been doing? Why did you shout like that? Look what you've made me do."

He pointed to the floor. The very old pair of tennis shoes which he wore were by this time generously soaked with the spilled water.

"Lor, Mr. Ukridge, sir, is that you?" said the red-headed man calmly. "I thought you was burglars."

A short bark from the other side of the kitchen door, followed by a renewal of the scratching, drew Mr. Beale's attention to his faithful hound.

"That's Bob," he said.

"I don't know what you call the brute," said Ukridge. "Come in and tie him up. And mind what you're doing with that gun. After you've finished with the dog, I should like a brief chat with you, laddie, if you can spare the time and have no other engagements."

Mr. Beale, having carefully deposited the gun against the wall and dropped a pair of very limp rabbits on the floor, proceeded to climb in through the window. This operation concluded, he stood to one side while the besieged garrison passed out by the same route.

"You will find me in the garden," said Ukridge coldly. "I've one or two little things to say to you."

Mr. Beale grinned affably. He seemed to be a man of equable temperament.

The cool air of the garden was grateful after the warmth of the kitchen. It was a pretty garden, or would have been if it had not been so neglected. I seemed to see myself sitting in a deck-chair on the lawn, smoking and looking through the trees at the harbour below. It was a spot, I felt, in which it would be an easy and a pleasant task to shape the plot of my novel. I was glad I had come. About now, outside my lodgings in town, a particularly foul barrel-organ would be settling down to work.

"Oh, there you are, Beale," said Ukridge, as the servitor appeared. "Now then, what have you to say?"

The hired man looked thoughtful for a moment, then said that it was a fine evening.

"Fine evening?" shouted Ukridge. "What on earth has that got to do with it? I want to know why you and Mrs. Beale were out when we arrived."

"The missus went to Axminster, Mr. Ukridge, sir."

"She had no right to go to Axminster. It isn't part of her duties to go gadding about to Axminster. I don't pay her enormous sums to go to Axminster. You knew I was coming this evening."

"No, sir."

"What!"

"No, sir."

"Beale," said Ukridge with studied calm, the strong man repressing himself. "One of us two is a fool."

"Yes, sir."

"Let us sift this matter to the bottom. You got my letter?"

"No, sir."

"My letter saying that I should arrive today. You didn't get it?"

"No, sir."

"Now, look here, Beale, this is absurd. I am certain that that letter was posted. I remember placing it in my pocket for that purpose. It is not there now. See. These are all the contents of my—well, I'm hanged."

He stood looking at the envelope which he had produced from his breast-pocket. A soft smile played over Mr. Beale's wooden face. He coughed.

"Beale," said Ukridge, "you—er—there seems to have been a mistake."

"Yes, sir."

"You are not so much to blame as I thought."

"No, sir."

There was a silence.

"Anyhow," said Ukridge in inspired tones, "I'll go and slay that infernal dog. I'll teach him to tear my door to pieces. Where's your gun, Beale?"

But better counsels prevailed, and the proceedings closed with a cold but pleasant little dinner, at which the spared mongrel came out unexpectedly strong with ingenious and diverting tricks.

V

BUCKLING TO

Sunshine, streaming into my bedroom through the open window, woke me next day as distant clocks were striking eight. It was a lovely morning, cool and fresh. The grass of the lawn, wet with dew, sparkled in the sun. A thrush, who knew all about early birds and their perquisites, was filling in the time before the arrival of the worm with a song or two, as he sat in the bushes. In the ivy a colony of sparrows were opening the day with brisk scuffling. On the gravel in front of the house lay the mongrel, Bob, blinking lazily.

The gleam of the sea through the trees turned my thoughts to bathing. I dressed quickly and went out. Bob rose to meet me, waving an absurdly long tail. The hatchet was definitely buried now. That little matter of the jug of water was forgotten.

A walk of five minutes down the hill brought me, accompanied by Bob, to the sleepy little town. I passed through the narrow street, and turned on to the beach, walking in the direction of the combination of pier and break-water which loomed up through the faint mist.

The tide was high, and, leaving my clothes to the care of Bob, who treated them as a handy bed, I dived into twelve feet of clear, cold water. As I swam, I compared it with the morning tub of London, and felt that I had done well to come with Ukridge to this pleasant spot. Not that I could rely on unbroken calm during the whole of my visit. I knew nothing of chicken-farming, but I was certain that Ukridge knew less. There would be some strenuous moments before that farm became a profitable commercial speculation. At the thought of Ukridge toiling on a hot afternoon to manage an undisciplined mob of fowls, I laughed, and swallowed a generous mouthful of salt water; and, turning, swam back to Bob and my clothes.

On my return, I found Ukridge, in his shirt sleeves and minus a collar, assailing a large ham. Mrs. Ukridge, looking younger and more child-like than ever in brown holland, smiled at me over the tea-pot.

"Hullo, old horse," bellowed Ukridge, "where have you been? Bathing? Hope it's made you feel fit for work, because we've got to buckle to this morning."

"The fowls have arrived, Mr. Garnet," said Mrs. Ukridge, opening her eyes till she looked like an astonished kitten. "*Such* a lot of them. They're making such a noise."

To support her statement there floated in through the window a cackling which for volume and variety beat anything I had ever heard. Judging from the noise, it seemed as if England had been drained of fowls and the entire tribe of them dumped into the yard of Ukridge's farm.

"There seems to have been no stint," I said.

"Quite a goodish few, aren't there?" said Ukridge complacently. "But that's what we want. No good starting on a small scale. The more you have, the bigger the profits."

"What sorts have you got mostly?" I asked, showing a professional interest.

"Oh, all sorts. My theory, laddie, is this. It doesn't matter a bit what kind we get, because they'll all lay; and if we sell settings of eggs, which we will, we'll merely say it's an unfortunate accident if they turn out mixed when hatched. Bless you, people don't mind what breed a fowl is, so long as it's got two legs and a beak. These dealer chaps were so infernally particular. 'Any Dorkings?' they said. 'All right,' I said, 'bring on your Dorkings.' 'Or perhaps you will require a few Minorcas?' 'Very well,' I said, 'unleash the Minorcas.' They were going on—they'd have gone on for hours—but I stopped 'em. 'Look here, my dear old college chum,' I said kindly but firmly to the manager johnny—decent old buck, with the manners of a marquess,—'look here,' I said, 'life is short, and we're neither of us as young as we used to be. Don't let us waste the golden hours playing guessing games. I want fowls. You sell fowls. So give me some of all sorts. Mix 'em up, laddie,' I said, 'mix 'em up.' And he has, by jove. You go into the yard and look at 'em. Beale has turned them out of their crates. There must be one of every breed ever invented."

"Where are you going to put them?"

"That spot we chose by the paddock. That's the place. Plenty of mud for them to scratch about in, and they can go into the field when they feel like it, and pick up worms, or whatever they feed on. We must rig them up some sort of shanty, I suppose, this morning. We'll go and tell 'em to send up some wire-netting and stuff from the town."

"Then we shall want hen-coops. We shall have to make those."

"Of course. So we shall. Millie, didn't I tell you that old Garnet was the man to think of things. I forgot the coops. We can't buy some, I suppose? On tick, of course."

"Cheaper to make them. Suppose we get a lot of boxes. Sugar boxes are as good as any. It won't take long to knock up a few coops."

Ukridge thumped the table with enthusiasm, upsetting his cup.

"Garny, old horse, you're a marvel. You think of everything. We'll buckle to right away, and get the whole place fixed up the same as mother makes it. What an infernal noise those birds are making. I suppose they don't feel at home in the yard. Wait till they see the A1 compact residential mansions we're going to put up for them. Finished breakfast? Then let's go out. Come along, Millie."

The red-headed Beale, discovered leaning in an attitude of thought on the yard gate and observing the feathered mob below with much interest, was roused from his reflections and despatched to the town for the wire and sugar boxes. Ukridge, taking his place at the gate, gazed at the fowls with the affectionate air of a proprietor.

"Well, they have certainly taken you at your word," I said, "as far as variety is concerned."

The man with the manners of a marquess seemed to have been at great pains to send a really representative selection of fowls. There were blue ones, black ones, white, grey, yellow, brown, big, little, Dorkings, Minorcas, Cochin Chinas, Bantams, Wyandottes. It was an imposing spectacle.

The Hired Man returned towards the end of the morning, preceded by a cart containing the necessary wire and boxes; and Ukridge, whose enthusiasm brooked no delay, started immediately the task of fashioning the coops, while I, assisted by Beale, draped the wire-netting about the chosen spot next to the paddock. There were little unpleasantnesses— once a roar of anguish told that Ukridge's hammer had found the wrong billet, and on another occasion my flannel trousers suffered on the wire—but the work proceeded steadily. By the middle of the afternoon, things were in a sufficiently advanced state to suggest to Ukridge the advisability of a halt for refreshments.

"That's the way to do it," he said, beaming through misty pince-nez over a long glass. "That is the stuff to administer to 'em! At this rate we shall have the place in corking condition before bedtime. Quiet efficiency—that's the wheeze! What do you think of those for coops, Beale?"

The Hired Man examined them woodenly.

"I've seen worse, sir."

He continued his examination.

"But not many," he added. Beale's passion for the truth had made him unpopular in three regiments.

"They aren't so bad," I said, "but I'm glad I'm not a fowl."

"So you ought to be," said Ukridge, "considering the way you've put up that wire. You'll have them strangling themselves."

In spite of earnest labour the housing arrangements of the fowls were still in an incomplete state at the end of the day. The details of the evening's work are preserved in a letter which I wrote that night to my friend Lickford.

". . . HAVE YOU EVER PLAYED A game called Pigs in Clover? We have just finished a merry bout of it, with hens instead of marbles, which has lasted for an hour and a half. We are all dead tired, except the Hired Man, who seems to be made of india-rubber. He has just gone for a stroll on the beach. Wants some exercise, I suppose. Personally, I feel as if I should never move again. You have no conception of the difficulty of rounding up fowls and getting them safely to bed. Having no proper place to put them, we were obliged to stow some of them in the cube sugar-boxes and the rest in the basement. It has only just occurred to me that they ought to have had perches to roost on. It didn't strike me before. I shan't mention it to Ukridge, or that indomitable man will start making some, and drag me into it, too. After all, a hen can rough it for one night, and if I did a stroke more work I should collapse.

"My idea was to do the thing on the slow but sure principle. That is to say, take each bird singly and carry it to bed. It would have taken some time, but there would have been no confusion. But you can imagine that that sort of thing would not appeal to Stanley Featherstonehaugh! He likes his manoeuvres to be on a large, dashing, Napoleonic scale. He said, 'Open the yard gate and let the blighters come out into the open; then sail in and drive them in mass formation through the back door into the basement.' It was a great idea, but there was one fatal flaw in it. It didn't allow for the hens scattering. We opened the gate, and out they all came like an audience coming out of a theatre. Then we closed in on them to bring off the big drive. For about thirty seconds it looked as if we might do it. Then Bob, the Hired Man's dog, an animal who likes to be in whatever's going on, rushed out of the house into the middle of them, barking. There was a perfect stampede, and Heaven only knows where some of those fowls are now. There was one in particular, a large yellow bird, which, I should imagine, is nearing London by this time.

The last I saw of it, it was navigating at the rate of knots in that direction, with Bob after it, barking his hardest. The fowl was showing a rare turn of speed and gaining rapidly. Presently Bob came back, panting, having evidently given the thing up. We, in the meantime, were chasing the rest of the birds all over the garden. The affair had now resolved itself into the course of action I had suggested originally, except that instead of collecting them quietly and at our leisure, we had to run miles for each one we captured. After a time we introduced some sort of system into it. Mrs. Ukridge stood at the door. We chased the hens and brought them in. Then, as we put each through into the basement, she shut the door on it. We also arranged Ukridge's sugar-box coops in a row, and when we caught a fowl we put it in the coop and stuck a board in front of it. By these strenuous means we gathered in about two-thirds of the lot. The rest are all over England. A few may be still in Dorsetshire, but I should not like to bet on it.

"So you see things are being managed on the up-to-date chicken farm on good, sound Ukridge principles. It is only the beginning. I look with confidence for further interesting events. I believe if Ukridge kept white mice he would manage to get feverish excitement out of it. He is at present lying on the sofa, smoking one of his infernal brand of cigars, drinking whisky and soda, and complaining with some bitterness because the whisky isn't as good as some he once tasted in Belfast. From the basement I can hear faintly the murmur of innumerable fowls."

VI

Mr. Garnet's Narrative—Has to Do With a Reunion

The day was Thursday, the date July the twenty-second. We had been chicken-farmers for a whole week, and things were beginning to settle down to a certain extent. The coops were finished. They were not masterpieces, and I have seen chickens pause before them in deep thought, as who should say, "Now what?" but they were coops within the meaning of the Act, and we induced hens to become tenants.

The hardest work had been the fixing of the wire-netting. This was the department of the Hired Man and myself, Ukridge holding himself proudly aloof. While Beale and I worked ourselves to a fever in the sun, the senior partner of the firm sat on a deck-chair in the shade, offering not unkindly criticism and advice and from time to time abusing his creditors, who were numerous. For we had hardly been in residence a day before he began to order in a vast supply of necessary and unnecessary things, all on credit. Some he got from the village, others from neighbouring towns. Axminster he laid heavily under contribution. He even went as far afield as Dorchester. He had a persuasive way with him, and the tradesmen seemed to treat him like a favourite son. The things began to pour in from all sides,—groceries, whisky, a piano, a gramophone, pictures. Also cigars in great profusion. He was not one of those men who want but little here below.

As regards the financial side of these transactions, his method was simple and masterly. If a tradesman suggested that a small cheque on account would not be taken amiss, as one or two sordid fellows did, he became pathetic.

"Confound it, sir," he would say with tears in his voice, laying a hand on the man's shoulders in a wounded way, "it's a trifle hard, when a gentleman comes to settle in your neighbourhood, that you should dun him for money before he has got the preliminary expenses about the house off his back." This sounded well, and suggested the disbursement of huge sums for rent. The fact that the house had been lent him rent free was kept with some care in the background. Having weakened the man with pathos, he would strike a sterner note. "A little more of this," he would go on, "and I'll close my account. Why, damme, in all my experience I've never heard anything like it!" Upon which the man would apologise, and go away, forgiven, with a large order for more goods.

By these statesmanlike methods he had certainly made the place very comfortable. I suppose we all realised that the things would have to be paid for some day, but the thought did not worry us.

"Pay?" bellowed Ukridge on the only occasion when I ventured to bring up the unpleasant topic, "of course we shall pay. Why not? I don't like to see this faint-hearted spirit in you, old horse. The money isn't coming in yet, I admit, but we must give it time. Soon we shall be turning over hundreds a week, hundreds! I'm in touch with all the big places,—Whiteley's, Harrod's, all the nibs. Here I am, I said to them, with a large chicken farm with all the modern improvements. You want eggs, old horses, I said: I supply them. I will let you have so many hundred eggs a week, I said; what will you give for them? Well, I'll admit their terms did not come up to my expectations altogether, but we must not sneer at small prices at first.

"When we get a connection, we shall be able to name our terms. It stands to reason, laddie. Have you ever seen a man, woman, or child who wasn't eating an egg or just going to eat an egg or just coming away from eating an egg? I tell you, the good old egg is the foundation of daily life. Stop the first man you meet in the street and ask him which he'd sooner lose, his egg or his wife, and see what he says! We're on to a good thing, Garny, my boy. Pass the whisky!"

The upshot of it was that the firms mentioned supplied us with a quantity of goods, agreeing to receive phantom eggs in exchange. This satisfied Ukridge. He had a faith in the laying power of his hens which would have flattered them if they could have known it. It might also have stimulated their efforts in that direction, which up to date were feeble.

It was now, as I have said, Thursday, the twenty-second of July,—a glorious, sunny morning, of the kind which Providence sends occasionally, simply in order to allow the honest smoker to take his after-breakfast pipe under ideal conditions. These are the pipes to which a man looks back in after years with a feeling of wistful reverence, pipes smoked in perfect tranquillity, mind and body alike at rest. It is over pipes like these that we dream our dreams, and fashion our masterpieces.

My pipe was behaving like the ideal pipe; and, as I strolled spaciously about the lawn, my novel was growing nobly. I had neglected my literary work for the past week, owing to the insistent claims of the fowls. I am not one of those men whose minds work in placid independence of the conditions of life. But I was making up for lost time now. With each blue cloud that left my lips and hung in the still air above me, striking scenes and freshets of sparkling dialogue rushed through my brain. Another uninterrupted half hour, and I have no doubt that I should have completed the framework of a novel which would have placed me in that select band of authors who have no christian names. Another half hour, and posterity would have known me as "Garnet."

But it was not to be.

"Stop her! Catch her, Garny, old horse!"

I had wandered into the paddock at the moment. I looked up. Coming towards me at her best pace was a small hen. I recognised her immediately. It was the disagreeable, sardonic-looking bird which Ukridge, on the strength of an alleged similarity of profile to his wife's nearest relative, had christened Aunt Elizabeth. A Bolshevist hen, always at the bottom of any disturbance in the fowl-run, a bird which ate its head off daily at our expense and bit the hands which fed it by resolutely declining to lay a single egg. Behind this fowl ran Bob, doing, as usual, the thing that he ought not to have done. Bob's wrong-headedness in the matter of our hens was a constant source of inconvenience. From the first, he had seemed to regard the laying-in of our stock purely in the nature of a tribute to his sporting tastes. He had a fixed idea that he was a hunting dog and that, recognising this, we had very decently provided him with the material for the chase.

Behind Bob came Ukridge. But a glance was enough to tell me that he was a negligible factor in the pursuit. He was not built for speed. Already the pace had proved too much for him, and he had appointed me his deputy, with full powers to act.

"After her, Garny, old horse! Valuable bird! Mustn't be lost!"

When not in a catalepsy of literary composition, I am essentially the man of action. I laid aside my novel for future reference, and we passed out of the paddock in the following order. First, Aunt Elizabeth, as fresh as paint, going well. Next, Bob, panting and obviously doubtful of his powers of staying the distance. Lastly, myself, determined, but wishing I were five years younger.

After the first field Bob, like the dilettante and unstable dog he was, gave it up, and sauntered off to scratch at a rabbit-hole with an insufferable air of suggesting that that was what he had come out for all the time. I continued to pound along doggedly. I was grimly resolute. I had caught Aunt Elizabeth's eye as she passed me, and the contempt in it had cut me to the quick. This bird despised me. I am not a violent or a quick-tempered man, but I have my self-respect. I will not be sneered at by hens. All the abstract desire for Fame which had filled my mind five minutes before was concentrated now on the task of capturing this supercilious bird.

We had been travelling down hill all this time, but at this point we crossed a road and the ground began to rise. I was in that painful condition which occurs when one has lost one's first wind and has not yet got one's second. I was hotter than I had ever been in my life.

Whether Aunt Elizabeth, too, was beginning to feel the effects of her run, or whether she did it out of the pure effrontery of her warped and unpleasant nature, I do not know; but she now slowed down to walk, and even began to peck in a tentative manner at the grass. Her behaviour infuriated me. I felt that I was being treated as a cipher. I vowed that this bird should realise yet, even if, as seemed probable, I burst in the process, that it was no light matter to be pursued by J. Garnet, author of "The Manoeuvres of Arthur," etc., a man of whose work so capable a judge as the Peebles *Advertiser* had said "Shows promise."

A judicious increase of pace brought me within a yard or two of my quarry. But Aunt Elizabeth, apparently distrait, had the situation well in hand. She darted from me with an amused chuckle, and moved off rapidly again up the hill.

I followed, but there was that within me that told me I had shot my bolt. The sun blazed down, concentrating its rays on my back to the exclusion of the surrounding scenery. It seemed to follow me about like a limelight.

We had reached level ground. Aunt Elizabeth had again slowed to a walk, and I was capable of no better pace. Very gradually I closed in. There was a high boxwood hedge in front of us; and, just as I came close enough once more to stake my all on a single grab, Aunt Elizabeth, with another of her sardonic chuckles, dived in head-foremost and struggled through in the mysterious way in which birds do get through hedges. The sound of her faint spinster-like snigger came to me as I stood panting, and roused me like a bugle. The next moment I too had plunged into the hedge.

I was in the middle of it, very hot, tired, and dirty, when from the other side I heard a sudden shout of "Mark over! Bird to the right!" and the next moment I found myself emerging with a black face and tottering knees on the gravel path of a private garden. Beyond the path was a croquet lawn, and on this lawn I perceived, as through a glass darkly, three figures. The mist cleared from my eyes, and I recognised two of them.

One was the middle-aged Irishman who had travelled down with us in the train. The other was his blue-eyed daughter.

The third member of the party was a man, a stranger to me. By some miracle of adroitness he had captured Aunt Elizabeth, and was holding her in spite of her protests in a workmanlike manner behind the wings.

VII

The Entente Cordiale is Sealed

There are moments and moments. The present one belonged to the more painful variety.

Even to my exhausted mind it was plain that there was a need here for explanations. An Irishman's croquet-lawn is his castle, and strangers cannot plunge in through hedges without inviting comment.

Unfortunately, speech was beyond me. I could have emptied a water-butt, laid down and gone to sleep, or melted ice with a touch of the finger, but I could not speak. The conversation was opened by the other man, in whose restraining hand Aunt Elizabeth now lay, outwardly resigned but inwardly, as I, who knew her haughty spirit, could guess, boiling with baffled resentment. I could see her looking out of the corner of her eye, trying to estimate the chances of getting in one good hard peck with her aquiline beak.

"Come right in," said the man pleasantly. "Don't knock."

I stood there, gasping. I was only too well aware that I presented a quaint appearance. I had removed my hat before entering the hedge, and my hair was full of twigs and other foreign substances. My face was moist and grimy. My mouth hung open. My legs felt as if they had ceased to belong to me.

"I must apol—. . ." I began, and ended the sentence with gulps.

The elderly gentleman looked at me with what seemed to be indignant surprise. His daughter appeared to my guilty conscience to be looking through me. Aunt Elizabeth sneered. The only friendly face was the man's. He regarded me with a kindly smile, as if I were some old friend who had dropped in unexpectedly.

"Take a long breath," he advised.

I took several, and felt better.

"I must apologise for this intrusion," I said successfully. "Unwarrantable" would have rounded off the sentence neatly, but I would not risk it. It would have been mere bravado to attempt unnecessary words of five syllables. I took in more breath. "The fact is, I did—didn't know there was a private garden beyond the hedge. If you will give me my hen. . ."

I stopped. Aunt Elizabeth was looking away, as if endeavouring to create an impression of having nothing to do with me. I am told by one who knows that hens cannot raise their eyebrows, not having any; but I am prepared to swear that at this moment Aunt Elizabeth raised hers. I will go further. She sniffed.

"Here you are," said the man. "Though it's hard to say good-bye."

He held out the hen to me, and at this point a hitch occurred. He did his part, the letting go, all right. It was in my department, the taking hold, that the thing was bungled. Aunt Elizabeth slipped from my grasp like an eel, stood for a moment eyeing me satirically with her head on one side, then fled and entrenched herself in some bushes at the end of the lawn.

There are times when the most resolute man feels that he can battle no longer with fate; when everything seems against him and the only course is a dignified retreat. But there is one thing essential to a dignified retreat. You must know the way out. It was the lack of that knowledge that kept me standing there, looking more foolish than anyone has ever looked since the world began. I could not retire by way of the hedge. If I could have leaped the hedge with a single debonair bound, that would have been satisfactory. But the hedge was high, and I did not feel capable at the moment of achieving a debonair bound over a footstool.

The man saved the situation. He seemed to possess that magnetic power over his fellows which marks the born leader. Under his command we became an organised army. The common object, the pursuit of the elusive Aunt Elizabeth, made us friends. In the first minute of the proceedings the Irishman was addressing me as "me dear boy," and the man, who had introduced himself as Mr. Chase—a lieutenant, I learned later, in His Majesty's Navy—was shouting directions to me by name. I have never assisted at any ceremony at which formality was so completely dispensed with. The ice was not merely broken; it was shivered into a million fragments.

"Go in and drive her out, Garnet," shouted Mr. Chase. "In my direction if you can. Look out on the left, Phyllis."

Even in that disturbing moment I could not help noticing his use of the Christian name. It seemed to me more than sinister. I did not like the idea of dashing young lieutenants in the senior service calling a girl Phyllis whose eyes had haunted me since I had first seen them.

Nevertheless, I crawled into the bushes and administered to Aunt Elizabeth a prod in the lower ribs—if hens have lower ribs. The more

I study hens, the more things they seem able to get along without—which abruptly disturbed her calm detachment. She shot out at the spot where Mr. Chase was waiting with his coat off, and was promptly enveloped in that garment and captured.

"The essence of strategy," observed Mr. Chase approvingly, "is surprise. A neat piece of work!"

I thanked him. He deprecated my thanks. He had, he said, only done his duty, as expected to by England. He then introduced me to the elderly Irishman, who was, it seemed, a professor at Dublin University, by name, Derrick. Whatever it was that he professed, it was something that did not keep him for a great deal of his time at the University. He informed me that he always spent his summers at Combe Regis.

"I was surprised to see you at Combe Regis," I said. "When you got out at Yeovil, I thought I had seen the last of you."

I think I am gifted beyond other men as regards the unfortunate turning of sentences.

"I meant," I added, "I was afraid I had."

"Ah, of course," he said, "you were in our carriage coming down. I was confident I had seen you before. I never forget a face."

"It would be a kindness," said Mr. Chase, "if you would forget Garnet's as now exhibited. You seem to have collected a good deal of the scenery coming through that hedge."

"I was wondering—" I said. "A wash—if I might—"

"Of course, me boy, of course," said the professor. "Tom, take Mr. Garnet off to your room, and then we'll have lunch. You'll stay to lunch, Mr. Garnet?"

I thanked him, commented on possible inconvenience to his arrangements, was overruled, and went off with my friend the lieutenant to the house. We imprisoned Aunt Elizabeth in the stables, to her profound indignation, gave directions for lunch to be served to her, and made our way to Mr. Chase's room.

"So you've met the professor before?" he said, hospitably laying out a change of raiment for me—we were fortunately much of a height and build.

"I have never spoken to him," I said. "We travelled down from London in the same carriage."

"He's a dear old boy, if you rub him the right way. But—I'm telling you this for your good and guidance; a man wants a chart in a strange sea—he can cut up rough. And, when he does, he goes off like a four-point-seven and the population for miles round climbs trees. I think, if I were you, I shouldn't mention Sir Edward Carson at lunch."

I promised that I would try to avoid the temptation.

"In fact, you'd better keep off Ireland altogether. It's the safest plan. Any other subject you like. Chatty remarks on Bimetallism would meet with his earnest attention. A lecture on What to do with the Cold Mutton would be welcomed. But not Ireland. Shall we do down?"

We got to know each other at lunch.

"Do you hunt hens," asked Tom Chase, who was mixing the salad—he was one of those men who seemed to do everything a shade better than anyone else—"for amusement or by your doctor's orders? Many doctors, I believe, insist on it."

"Neither," I said, "and especially not for amusement. The fact is, I've been lured down here by a friend of mine who has started a chicken farm—"

I was interrupted. All three of them burst out laughing. Tom Chase allowed the vinegar to trickle on to the cloth, missing the salad-bowl by a clear two inches.

"You don't mean to tell us," he said, "that you really come from the one and only chicken farm? Why, you're the man we've all been praying to meet for days past. You're the talk of the town. If you can call Combe Regis a town. Everybody is discussing you. Your methods are new and original, aren't they?"

"Probably. Ukridge knows nothing about fowls. I know less. He considers it an advantage. He says our minds ought to be unbiassed."

"Ukridge!" said the professor. "That was the name old Dawlish, the grocer, said. I never forget a name. He is the gentleman who lectures on the management of poultry? You do not?"

I hastened to disclaim any such feat. I had never really approved of these infernal talks on the art of chicken-farming which Ukridge had dropped into the habit of delivering when anybody visited our farm. I admit that it was a pleasing spectacle to see my managing director in a pink shirt without a collar and very dirty flannel trousers lecturing the intelligent native; but I had a feeling that the thing tended to expose our ignorance to men who had probably had to do with fowls from their cradle up.

"His lectures are very popular," said Phyllis Derrick with a little splutter of mirth.

P.G. WODEHOUSE

"He enjoys them," I said.

"Look here, Garnet," said Tom Chase, "I hope you won't consider all these questions impertinent, but you've no notion of the thrilling interest we all take—at a distance—in your farm. We have been talking of nothing else for a week. I have dreamed of it three nights running. Is Mr. Ukridge doing this as a commercial speculation, or is he an eccentric millionaire?"

"He's not a millionaire yet, but I believe he intends to be one shortly, with the assistance of the fowls. But you mustn't look on me as in any way responsible for the arrangements at the farm. I am merely a labourer. The brainwork of the business lies in Ukridge's department. As a matter of fact, I came down here principally in search of golf."

"Golf?" said Professor Derrick, with the benevolent approval of the enthusiast towards a brother. "I'm glad you play golf. We must have a round together."

"As soon as ever my professional duties will permit," I said gratefully.

There was croquet after lunch,—a game of which I am a poor performer. Phyllis Derrick and I played the professor and Tom Chase. Chase was a little better than myself; the professor, by dint of extreme earnestness and care, managed to play a fair game; and Phyllis was an expert.

"I was reading a book," she said, as we stood together watching the professor shaping at his ball at the other end of the lawn, "by an author of the same surname as you, Mr. Garnet. Is he a relation of yours?"

"My name is Jeremy, Miss Derrick."

"Oh, you wrote it?" She turned a little pink. "Then you must have—oh, nothing."

"I couldn't help it, I'm afraid."

"Did you know what I was going to say?"

"I guessed. You were going to say that I must have heard your criticisms in the train. You were very lenient, I thought."

"I didn't like your heroine."

"No. What is a 'creature,' Miss Derrick?"

"Pamela in your book is a 'creature,'" she replied unsatisfactorily.

Shortly after this the game came somehow to an end. I do not understand the intricacies of croquet. But Phyllis did something brilliant and remarkable with the balls, and we adjourned for tea. The sun was setting as I left to return to the farm, with Aunt Elizabeth stored neatly in a basket in my hand. The air was deliciously cool, and full of that strange quiet which follows soothingly on the skirts of a broiling midsummer afternoon. Far away, seeming to come from another world, a sheep-bell tinkled, deepening the silence. Alone in a sky of the palest blue there gleamed a small, bright star.

I addressed this star.

"She was certainly very nice to me. Very nice indeed." The star said nothing.

"On the other hand, I take it that, having had a decent up-bringing, she would have been equally polite to any other man whom she had happened to meet at her father's house. Moreover, I don't feel altogether easy in my mind about that naval chap. I fear the worst."

The star winked.

"He calls her Phyllis," I said.

"Charawk!" chuckled Aunt Elizabeth from her basket, in that beastly cynical, satirical way which has made her so disliked by all right-thinking people.

VIII

A Little Dinner at Ukridge's

E dwin comes today," said Mrs. Ukridge.

"And the Derricks," said Ukridge, sawing at the bread in his energetic way. "Don't forget the Derricks, Millie."

"No, dear. Mrs. Beale is going to give us a very nice dinner. We talked it over yesterday."

"Who is Edwin?" I asked.

We were finishing breakfast on the second morning after my visit to the Derricks. I had related my adventures to the staff of the farm on my return, laying stress on the merits of our neighbours and their interest in our doings, and the Hired Retainer had been sent off next morning with a note from Mrs. Ukridge inviting them to look over the farm and stay to dinner.

"Edwin?" said Ukridge. "Oh, beast of a cat."

"Oh, Stanley!" said Mrs. Ukridge plaintively. "He's not. He's such a dear, Mr. Garnet. A beautiful, pure-bred Persian. He has taken prizes."

"He's always taking something. That's why he didn't come down with us."

"A great, horrid, *beast* of a dog bit him, Mr. Garnet. And poor Edwin had to go to a cats' hospital."

"And I hope," said Ukridge, "the experience will do him good. Sneaked a dog's dinner, Garnet, under his very nose, if you please. Naturally the dog lodged a protest."

"I'm so afraid that he will be frightened of Bob. He will be very timid, and Bob's so boisterous. Isn't he, Mr. Garnet?"

"That's all right," said Ukridge. "Bob won't hurt him, unless he tries to steal his dinner. In that case we will have Edwin made into a rug."

"Stanley doesn't like Edwin," said Mrs. Ukridge, sadly.

Edwin arrived early in the afternoon, and was shut into the kitchen. He struck me as a handsome cat, but nervous.

The Derricks followed two hours later. Mr. Chase was not of the party.

"Tom had to go to London," explained the professor, "or he would have been delighted to come. It was a disappointment to the boy, for he wanted to see the farm."

"He must come some other time," said Ukridge. "We invite inspection. Look here," he broke off suddenly—we were nearing the fowl-run now, Mrs. Ukridge walking in front with Phyllis Derrick—"were you ever at Bristol?"

"Never, sir," said the professor.

"Because I knew just such another fat little buffer there a few years ago. Gay old bird, he was. He—"

"This is the fowl-run, professor," I broke in, with a moist, tingling feeling across my forehead and up my spine. I saw the professor stiffen as he walked, while his face deepened in colour. Ukridge's breezy way of expressing himself is apt to electrify the stranger.

"You will notice the able way—ha! ha!—in which the wire-netting is arranged," I continued feverishly. "Took some doing, that. By Jove, yes. It was hot work. Nice lot of fowls, aren't they? Rather a mixed lot, of course. Ha! ha! That's the dealer's fault though. We are getting quite a number of eggs now. Hens wouldn't lay at first. Couldn't make them."

I babbled on, till from the corner of my eye I saw the flush fade from the professor's face and his back gradually relax its poker-like attitude. The situation was saved for the moment but there was no knowing what further excesses Ukridge might indulge in. I managed to draw him aside as we went through the fowl-run, and expostulated.

"For goodness sake, be careful," I whispered. "You've no notion how touchy he is."

"But *I* said nothing," he replied, amazed.

"Hang it, you know, nobody likes to be called a fat little buffer to his face."

"What! My dear old man, nobody minds a little thing like that. We can't be stilted and formal. It's ever so much more friendly to relax and be chummy."

Here we rejoined the others, and I was left with a leaden foreboding of gruesome things in store. I knew what manner of man Ukridge was when he relaxed and became chummy. Friendships of years' standing had failed to survive the test.

For the time being, however, all went well. In his role of lecturer he offended no one, and Phyllis and her father behaved admirably. They received his strangest theories without a twitch of the mouth.

"Ah," the professor would say, "now is that really so? Very interesting indeed."

Only once, when Ukridge was describing some more than usually original device for the furthering of the interests of his fowls, did a slight spasm disturb Phyllis's look of attentive reverence.

"And you have really had no previous experience in chicken-farming?" she said.

"None," said Ukridge, beaming through his glasses. "Not an atom. But I can turn my hand to anything, you know. Things seem to come naturally to me somehow."

"I see," said Phyllis.

It was while matters were progressing with this beautiful smoothness that I observed the square form of the Hired Retainer approaching us. Somehow—I cannot say why—I had a feeling that he came with bad news. Perhaps it was his air of quiet satisfaction which struck me as ominous.

"Beg pardon, Mr. Ukridge, sir."

Ukridge was in the middle of a very eloquent excursus on the feeding of fowls, a subject on which he held views of his own as ingenious as they were novel. The interruption annoyed him.

"Well, Beale," he said, "what is it?"

"That there cat, sir, what came today."

"Oh, Beale," cried Mrs. Ukridge in agitation, "*what* has happened?"

"Having something to say to the missis—"

"What has happened? Oh, Beale, don't say that Edwin has been hurt? Where is he? Oh, *poor* Edwin!"

"Having something to say to the missis—"

"If Bob has bitten him I hope he had his nose *well* scratched," said Mrs. Ukridge vindictively.

"Having something to say to the missis," resumed the Hired Retainer tranquilly, "I went into the kitchen ten minutes back. The cat was sitting on the mat."

Beale's narrative style closely resembled that of a certain book I had read in my infancy. I wish I could remember its title. It was a well-written book.

"Yes, Beale, yes?" said Mrs. Ukridge. "Oh, do go on."

"'Hullo, puss,' I says to him, 'and 'ow are *you*, sir?' 'Be careful,' says the missis. ''E's that timid,' she says, 'you wouldn't believe,' she says. ''E's only just settled down, as you may say,' she says. 'Ho, don't you fret,' I says to her, "im and me understands each other. 'Im and me,' I says, 'is old friends. 'E's my dear old pal, Corporal Banks.' She grinned at that, ma'am, Corporal Banks being a man we'd 'ad many a 'earty laugh at in the old days. 'E was, in a manner of speaking, a joke between us."

"Oh, do—go—on, Beale. What has happened to Edwin?"

The Hired Retainer proceeded in calm, even tones.

"We was talking there, ma'am, when Bob, what had followed me unknown, trotted in. When the cat ketched sight of 'im sniffing about, there was such a spitting and swearing as you never 'eard; and blowed," said Mr. Beale amusedly, "blowed if the old cat didn't give one jump, and move in quick time up the chimney, where 'e now remains, paying no 'eed to the missis' attempts to get him down again."

Sensation, as they say in the reports.

"But he'll be cooked," cried Phyllis, open-eyed.

"No, he won't. Nor will our dinner. Mrs. Beale always lets the kitchen fire out during the afternoon. And how she's going to light it with that—"

There was a pause while one might count three. It was plain that the speaker was struggling with himself.

"—that cat," he concluded safely, "up the chimney? It's a cold dinner we'll get tonight, if that cat doesn't come down."

The professor's face fell. I had remarked on the occasion when I had lunched with him his evident fondness for the pleasures of the table. Cold impromptu dinners were plainly not to his taste.

We went to the kitchen in a body. Mrs. Beale was standing in front of the empty grate, making seductive cat-noises up the chimney.

"What's all this, Mrs. Beale?" said Ukridge.

"He won't come down, sir, not while he thinks Bob's about. And how I'm to cook dinner for five with him up the chimney I don't see, sir."

"Prod at him with a broom handle, Mrs. Beale," said Ukridge.

"Oh, don't hurt poor Edwin," said Mrs. Ukridge.

"I 'ave tried that, sir, but I can't reach him, and I'm only bin and drove 'im further up. What must be," added Mrs. Beale philosophically, "must be. He may come down of his own accord in the night. Bein' 'ungry."

"Then what we must do," said Ukridge in a jovial manner, which to me at least seemed out of place, "is to have a regular, jolly picnic-dinner, what? Whack up whatever we have in the larder, and eat that."

"A regular, jolly picnic-dinner," repeated the professor gloomily. I could read what was passing in his mind,—remorse for having come at all, and a faint hope that it might not be too late to back out of it.

"That will be splendid," said Phyllis.

P.G. WODEHOUSE

"Er, I think, my dear sir," said her father, "it would be hardly fair for us to give any further trouble to Mrs. Ukridge and yourself. If you will allow me, therefore, I will—"

Ukridge became gushingly hospitable. He refused to think of allowing his guests to go empty away. He would be able to whack up something, he said. There was quite a good deal of the ham left. He was sure. He appealed to me to endorse his view that there was a tin of sardines and part of a cold fowl and plenty of bread and cheese.

"And after all," he said, speaking for the whole company in the generous, comprehensive way enthusiasts have, "what more do we want in weather like this? A nice, light, cold, dinner is ever so much better for us than a lot of hot things."

We strolled out again into the garden, but somehow things seemed to drag. Conversation was fitful, except on the part of Ukridge, who continued to talk easily on all subjects, unconscious of the fact that the party was depressed and at least one of his guests rapidly becoming irritable. I watched the professor furtively as Ukridge talked on, and that ominous phrase of Mr. Chase's concerning four-point-seven guns kept coming into my mind. If Ukridge were to tread on any of his pet corns, as he might at any minute, there would be an explosion. The snatching of the dinner from his very mouth, as it were, and the substitution of a bread-and-cheese and sardines menu had brought him to the frame of mind when men turn and rend their nearest and dearest.

The sight of the table, when at length we filed into the dining room, sent a chill through me. It was a meal for the very young or the very hungry. The uncompromising coldness and solidity of the viands was enough to appall a man conscious that his digestion needed humouring. A huge cheese faced us in almost a swashbuckling way. I do not know how else to describe it. It wore a blatant, rakish, *nemo-me-impune-lacessit* air, and I noticed that the professor shivered slightly as he saw it. Sardines, looking more oily and uninviting than anything I had ever seen, appeared in their native tin beyond the loaf of bread. There was a ham, in its third quarter, and a chicken which had suffered heavily during a previous visit to the table. Finally, a black bottle of whisky stood grimly beside Ukridge's plate. The professor looked the sort of man who drank claret of a special year, or nothing.

We got through the meal somehow, and did our best to delude ourselves into the idea that it was all great fun; but it was a shallow pretence. The professor was very silent by the time we had finished.

Ukridge had been terrible. The professor had forced himself to be genial. He had tried to talk. He had told stories. And when he began one—his stories would have been the better for a little more briskness and condensation—Ukridge almost invariably interrupted him, before he had got half way through, without a word of apology, and started on some anecdote of his own. He furthermore disagreed with nearly every opinion the professor expressed. It is true that he did it all in such a perfectly friendly way, and was obviously so innocent of any intention of giving offence, that another man—or the same man at a better meal—might have overlooked the matter. But the professor, robbed of his good dinner, was at the stage when he had to attack somebody. Every moment I had been expecting the storm to burst.

It burst after dinner.

We were strolling in the garden, when some demon urged Ukridge, apropos of the professor's mention of Dublin, to start upon the Irish question. I had been expecting it momentarily, but my heart seemed to stand still when it actually arrived.

Ukridge probably knew less about the Irish question than any male adult in the kingdom, but he had boomed forth some very positive opinions of his own on the subject before I could get near enough to him to whisper a warning. When I did, I suppose I must have whispered louder than I had intended, for the professor heard me, and my words acted as the match to the powder.

"He's touchy about Ireland, is he?" he thundered. "Drop it, is it? And why? Why, sir? I'm one of the best tempered men that ever came from Dublin, let me tell you, and I will not stay here to be insulted by the insinuation that I cannot discuss Ireland as calmly as any one in this company or out of it. Touchy about Ireland, is it? Touchy—?"

"But, professor—"

"Take your hand off my arm, Mr. Garnet. I will not be treated like a child. I am as competent to discuss the affairs of Ireland without heat as any man, let me tell you."

"Father—"

"And let me tell you, Mr. Ukridge, that I consider your opinions poisonous. Poisonous, sir. And you know nothing whatever about the subject, sir. Every word you say betrays your profound ignorance. I don't wish to see you or to speak to you again. Understand that, sir. Our acquaintance began today, and it will cease today. Good-night to you, sir. Come, Phyllis, me dear. Mrs. Ukridge, good-night."

IX

Dies Irae

W hy is it, I wonder, that stories of Retribution calling at the wrong address strike us as funny instead of pathetic? I myself had been amused by them many a time. In a book which I had read only a few days before our cold-dinner party a shop-woman, annoyed with an omnibus conductor, had thrown a superannuated orange at him. It had found its billet not on him but on a perfectly inoffensive spectator. The missile, said the writer, "'it a young copper full in the hyeball." I had enjoyed this when I read it, but now that Fate had arranged a precisely similar situation, with myself in the role of the young copper, the fun of the thing appealed to me not at all.

It was Ukridge who was to blame for the professor's regrettable explosion and departure, and he ought by all laws of justice to have suffered for it. As it was, I was the only person materially affected. It did not matter to Ukridge. He did not care twopence one way or the other. If the professor were friendly, he was willing to talk to him by the hour on any subject, pleasant or unpleasant. If, on the other hand, he wished to have nothing more to do with us, it did not worry him. He was content to let him go. Ukridge was a self-sufficing person.

But to me it was a serious matter. More than serious. If I have done my work as historian with an adequate degree of skill, the reader should have gathered by this time the state of my feelings.

> "*I did not love as others do:*
> *None ever did that I've heard tell of.*
> *My passion was a by-word through*
> *The town she was, of course, the belle of.*"

At least it was—fortunately—not quite that; but it was certainly genuine and most disturbing, and it grew with the days. Somebody with a taste for juggling with figures might write a very readable page or so of statistics in connection with the growth of love. In some cases it is, I believe, slow. In my own I can only say that Jack's beanstalk was a backward plant in comparison. It is true that we had not seen a great deal of one another, and that, when we had met, our interview had been brief and our conversation conventional; but it is the intervals between the meeting that do the real damage. Absence—I do not claim the thought as my own—makes the heart grow fonder. And now, thanks to Ukridge's amazing idiocy, a barrier had been thrust between us. Lord knows, the business of fishing for a girl's heart is sufficiently difficult and delicate without the addition of needless obstacles. To cut out the naval miscreant under equal conditions would have been a task ample enough for my modest needs. It was terrible to have to re-establish myself in the good graces of the professor before I could so much as begin to dream of Phyllis. Ukridge gave me no balm.

"Well, after all," he said, when I pointed out to him quietly but plainly my opinion of his tactlessness, "what does it matter? Old Derrick isn't the only person in the world. If he doesn't want to know us, laddie, we just jolly well pull ourselves together and stagger along without him. It's quite possible to be happy without knowing old Derrick. Millions of people are going about the world at this moment, singing like larks out of pure light-heartedness, who don't even know of his existence. And, as a matter of fact, old horse, we haven't time to waste making friends and being the social pets. Too much to do on the farm. Strict business is the watchword, my boy. We must be the keen, tense men of affairs, or, before we know where we are, we shall find ourselves right in the gumbo.

"I've noticed, Garny, old horse, that you haven't been the whale for work lately that you might be. You must buckle to, laddie. There must be no slackness. We are at a critical stage. On our work now depends the success of the speculation. Look at those damned cocks. They're always fighting. Heave a stone at them, laddie, while you're up. What's the matter with you? You seem pipped. Can't get the novel off your chest, or what? You take my tip and give your brain a rest. Nothing like manual labour for clearing the brain. All the doctors say so. Those coops ought to be painted today or tomorrow. Mind you, I think old Derrick would be all right if one persevered—"

"—and didn't call him a fat little buffer and contradict everything he said and spoil all his stories by breaking in with chestnuts of your own in the middle," I interrupted with bitterness.

"My dear old son, he didn't mind being called a fat little buffer. You keep harping on that. It's no discredit to a man to be a fat little buffer. Some of the noblest men I have met have been fat little buffers. What was the matter with old Derrick was a touch of liver. I said to myself, when I saw him eating cheese, 'that fellow's going to have a nasty shooting pain sooner or later.' I say, laddie, just heave another rock or two at those cocks, will you. They'll slay each other."

I had hoped, fearing the while that there was not much chance of such a thing happening, that the professor might get over his feeling of injury during the night and be as friendly as ever next day. But he was evidently a man who had no objection whatever to letting the sun go down upon his wrath, for when I met him on the following morning on the beach, he cut me in the most uncompromising manner.

Phyllis was with him at the time, and also another girl, who was, I supposed, from the strong likeness between them, her sister. She had the same mass of soft brown hair. But to me she appeared almost commonplace in comparison.

It is never pleasant to be cut dead, even when you have done something to deserve it. It is like treading on nothing where one imagined a stair to be. In the present instance the pang was mitigated to a certain extent— not largely—by the fact that Phyllis looked at me. She did not move her head, and I could not have declared positively that she moved her eyes; but nevertheless she certainly looked at me. It was something. She seemed to say that duty compelled her to follow her father's lead, and that the act must not be taken as evidence of any personal animus.

That, at least, was how I read off the message.

Two days later I met Mr. Chase in the village.

"Hullo, so you're back," I said.

"You've discovered my secret," he admitted; "will you have a cigar or a cocoanut?"

There was a pause.

"Trouble I hear, while I was away," he said.

I nodded.

"The man I live with, Ukridge, did what you warned me against. Touched on the Irish question."

"Home Rule?"

"He mentioned it among other things."

"And the professor went off?"

"Like a bomb."

"He would. So now you have parted brass rags. It's a pity."

I agreed. I am glad to say that I suppressed the desire to ask him to use his influence, if any, with Mr. Derrick to effect a reconciliation. I felt that I must play the game. To request one's rival to give one assistance in the struggle, to the end that he may be the more readily cut out, can hardly be considered cricket.

"I ought not to be speaking to you, you know," said Mr. Chase. "You're under arrest."

"He's still—?" I stopped for a word.

"Very much so. I'll do what I can."

"It's very good of you."

"But the time is not yet ripe. He may be said at present to be simmering down."

"I see. Thanks. Good-bye."

"So long."

And Mr. Chase walked on with long strides to the Cob.

The days passed slowly. I saw nothing more of Phyllis or her sister. The professor I met once or twice on the links. I had taken earnestly to golf in this time of stress. Golf is the game of disappointed lovers. On the other hand, it does not follow that because a man is a failure as a lover he will be any good at all on the links. My game was distinctly poor at first. But a round or two put me back into my proper form, which is fair.

The professor's demeanour at these accidental meetings on the links was a faithful reproduction of his attitude on the beach. Only by a studied imitation of the Absolute Stranger did he show that he had observed my presence.

Once or twice, after dinner, when Ukridge was smoking one of his special cigars while Mrs. Ukridge nursed Edwin (now moving in society once more, and in his right mind), I lit my pipe and walked out across the fields through the cool summer night till I came to the hedge that shut off the Derrick's grounds. Not the hedge through which I had made my first entrance, but another, lower, and nearer the house. Standing there under the shade of a tree I could see the lighted windows of the drawing-room. Generally there was music inside, and, the windows being opened on account of the warmth of the night, I was able to make myself a little more miserable by hearing Phyllis sing. It deepened the feeling of banishment.

I shall never forget those furtive visits. The intense stillness of the night, broken by an occasional rustling in the grass or the hedge; the smell of the flowers in the garden beyond; the distant drone of the sea.

"God makes sech nights, all white and still,
Fur'z you to look and listen."

Another day had generally begun before I moved from my hiding-place, and started for home, surprised to find my limbs stiff and my clothes bathed with dew.

X

I Enlist the Services of a Minion

I t would be interesting to know to what extent the work of authors is influenced by their private affairs. If life is flowing smoothly, are the novels they write in that period of content coloured with optimism? And if things are running crosswise, do they work off the resultant gloom on their faithful public? If, for instance, Mr. W. W. Jacobs had toothache, would he write like Hugh Walpole? If Maxim Gorky were invited to lunch by Trotsky, to meet Lenin, would he sit down and dash off a trifle in the vein of Stephen Leacock? Probably the eminent have the power of detaching their writing self from their living, work-a-day self; but, for my own part, the frame of mind in which I now found myself had a disastrous effect on my novel that was to be. I had designed it as a light comedy effort. Here and there a page or two to steady the reader and show him what I could do in the way of pathos if I cared to try; but in the main a thing of sunshine and laughter. But now great slabs of gloom began to work themselves into the scheme of it. A magnificent despondency became its keynote. It would not do. I felt that I must make a resolute effort to shake off my depression. More than ever the need of conciliating the professor was borne in upon me. Day and night I spurred my brain to think of some suitable means of engineering a reconciliation.

In the meantime I worked hard among the fowls, drove furiously on the links, and swam about the harbour when the affairs of the farm did not require my attention.

Things were not going well on our model chicken farm. Little accidents marred the harmony of life in the fowl-run. On one occasion a hen—not Aunt Elizabeth, I am sorry to say,—fell into a pot of tar, and came out an unspeakable object. Ukridge put his spare pair of tennis shoes in the incubator to dry them, and permanently spoiled the future of half-a-dozen eggs which happened to have got there first. Chickens kept straying into the wrong coops, where they got badly pecked by the residents. Edwin slew a couple of Wyandottes, and was only saved from execution by the tears of Mrs. Ukridge.

In spite of these occurrences, however, his buoyant optimism never deserted Ukridge.

"After all," he said, "What's one bird more or less? Yes, I know I made a fuss when that beast of a cat lunched off those two, but that was simply the principle of the thing. I'm not going to pay large sums for chickens purely in order that a cat which I've never liked can lunch well. Still, we've plenty left, and the eggs are coming in better now, though we've still a deal of leeway to make up yet in that line. I got a letter from Whiteley's this morning asking when my first consignment was going to arrive. You know, these people make a mistake in hurrying a man. It annoys him. It irritates him. When we really get going, Garny, my boy, I shall drop Whiteley's. I shall cut them out of my list and send my eggs to their trade rivals. They shall have a sharp lesson. It's a little hard. Here am I, worked to death looking after things down here, and these men have the impertinence to bother me about their wretched business. Come in and have a drink, laddie, and let's talk it over."

It was on the morning after this that I heard him calling me in a voice in which I detected agitation. I was strolling about the paddock, as was my habit after breakfast, thinking about Phyllis and trying to get my novel into shape. I had just framed a more than usually murky scene for use in the earlier part of the book, when Ukridge shouted to me from the fowl-run.

"Garny, come here. I want you to see the most astounding thing."

"What's the matter?" I asked.

"Blast if I know. Look at those chickens. They've been doing that for the last half-hour."

I inspected the chickens. There was certainly something the matter with them. They were yawning—broadly, as if we bored them. They stood about singly and in groups, opening and shutting their beaks. It was an uncanny spectacle.

"What's the matter with them?"

"Can a chicken get a fit of the blues?" I asked. "Because if so, that's what they've got. I never saw a more bored-looking lot of birds."

"Oh, do look at that poor little brown one by the coop," said Mrs. Ukridge sympathetically; "I'm sure it's not well. See, it's lying down. What *can* be the matter with it?"

"I tell you what we'll do," said Ukridge. "We'll ask Beale. He once lived with an aunt who kept fowls. He'll know all about it. Beale!"

No answer.

"Beale!!"

A sturdy form in shirt-sleeves appeared through the bushes, carrying a boot. We seemed to have interrupted him in the act of cleaning it.

"Beale, you know all about fowls. What's the matter with these chickens?"

The Hired Retainer examined the blasé birds with a wooden expression on his face.

"Well?" said Ukridge.

"The 'ole thing 'ere," said the Hired Retainer, "is these 'ere fowls have been and got the roop."

I had never heard of the disease before, but it sounded bad.

"Is that what makes them yawn like that?" said Mrs. Ukridge.

"Yes, ma'am."

"Poor things!"

"Yes, ma'am."

"And have they all got it?"

"Yes, ma'am."

"What ought we to do?" asked Ukridge.

"Well, my aunt, sir, when 'er fowls 'ad the roop, she gave them snuff."

"Give them snuff, she did," he repeated, with relish, "every morning."

"Snuff!" said Mrs. Ukridge.

"Yes, ma'am. She give 'em snuff till their eyes bubbled."

Mrs. Ukridge uttered a faint squeak at this vivid piece of word-painting.

"And did it cure them?" asked Ukridge.

"No, sir," responded the expert soothingly.

"Oh, go away, Beale, and clean your beastly boots," said Ukridge. "You're no use. Wait a minute. Who would know about this infernal roop thing? One of those farmer chaps would, I suppose. Beale, go off to the nearest farmer, and give him my compliments, and ask him what he does when his fowls get the roop."

"Yes, sir."

"No, I'll go, Ukridge," I said. "I want some exercise."

I whistled to Bob, who was investigating a mole-heap in the paddock, and set off in the direction of the village of Up Lyme to consult Farmer Leigh on the matter. He had sold us some fowls shortly after our arrival, so might be expected to feel a kindly interest in their ailing families.

The path to Up Lyme lies across deep-grassed meadows. At intervals it passes over a stream by means of a footbridge. The stream curls through the meadows like a snake.

And at the first of these bridges I met Phyllis.

I came upon her quite suddenly. The other end of the bridge was hidden from my view. I could hear somebody coming through the grass, but not till I was on the bridge did I see who it was. We reached the bridge simultaneously. She was alone. She carried a sketching-block. All nice girls sketch a little.

There was room for one alone on the footbridge, and I drew back to let her pass.

It being the privilege of woman to make the first sign of recognition, I said nothing. I merely lifted my hat in a non-committing fashion.

"Are you going to cut me, I wonder?" I said to myself. She answered the unspoken question as I hoped it would be answered.

"Mr. Garnet," she said, stopping at the end of the bridge. A pause.

"I couldn't tell you so before, but I am so sorry this has happened."

"Oh, thanks awfully," I said, realising as I said it the miserable inadequacy of the English language. At a crisis when I would have given a month's income to have said something neat, epigrammatic, suggestive, yet withal courteous and respectful, I could only find a hackneyed, unenthusiastic phrase which I should have used in accepting an invitation from a bore to lunch with him at his club.

"Of course you understand my friends—must be my father's friends."

"Yes," I said gloomily, "I suppose so."

"So you must not think me rude if I—I—"

"Cut me," said I, with masculine coarseness.

"Don't seem to see you," said she, with feminine delicacy, "when I am with my father. You will understand?"

"I shall understand."

"You see,"—she smiled—"you are under arrest, as Tom says."

Tom!

"I see," I said.

"Good-bye."

"Good-bye."

I watched her out of sight, and went on to interview Mr. Leigh.

We had a long and intensely uninteresting conversation about the maladies to which chickens are subject. He was verbose and reminiscent. He took me over his farm, pointing out as we went Dorkings with pasts, and Cochin Chinas which he had cured of diseases generally fatal on, as far as I could gather, Christian Science principles.

I left at last with instructions to paint the throats of the stricken birds with turpentine—a task imagination boggled at, and one which I proposed to leave exclusively to Ukridge and the Hired Retainer—and also a slight headache. A visit to the Cob would, I thought, do me good. I had missed my bathe that morning, and was in need of a breath of sea-air.

It was high-tide, and there was deep water on three sides of the Cob.

In a small boat in the offing Professor Derrick appeared, fishing. I had seen him engaged in this pursuit once or twice before. His only companion was a gigantic boatman, by name Harry Hawk, possibly a descendant of the gentleman of that name who went to Widdicombe Fair with Bill Brewer and old Uncle Tom Cobley and all on a certain memorable occasion, and assisted at the fatal accident to Tom Pearse's grey mare.

I sat on the seat at the end of the Cob and watched the professor. It was an instructive sight, an object-lesson to those who hold that optimism has died out of the race. I had never seen him catch a fish. He never looked to me as if he were at all likely to catch a fish. Yet he persevered.

There are few things more restful than to watch some one else busy under a warm sun. As I sat there, my pipe drawing nicely as the result of certain explorations conducted that morning with a straw, my mind ranged idly over large subjects and small. I thought of love and chicken-farming. I mused on the immortality of the soul and the deplorable speed at which two ounces of tobacco disappeared. In the end I always returned to the professor. Sitting, as I did, with my back to the beach, I could see nothing but his boat. It had the ocean to itself.

I began to ponder over the professor. I wondered dreamily if he were very hot. I tried to picture his boyhood. I speculated on his future, and the pleasure he extracted from life.

It was only when I heard him call out to Hawk to be careful, when a movement on the part of that oarsman set the boat rocking, that I began to weave romances round him in which I myself figured.

But, once started, I progressed rapidly. I imagined a sudden upset. Professor struggling in water. Myself (heroically): "Courage! I'm coming!" A few rapid strokes. Saved! Sequel, a subdued professor, dripping salt water and tears of gratitude, urging me to become his son-in-law. That sort of thing happened in fiction. It was a shame that it should not happen in real life. In my hot youth I once had seven stories in seven weekly penny papers in the same month, all dealing with a situation of the kind. Only the details differed. In "Not really a Coward" Vincent Devereux had rescued the earl's daughter from a fire, whereas in "Hilda's Hero" it was the peppery old father whom Tom Slingsby saved. Singularly enough, from drowning. In other words, I, a very mediocre scribbler, had effected seven times in a single month what the Powers of the Universe could not manage once, even on the smallest scale.

IT WAS PRECISELY THREE MINUTES to twelve—I had just consulted my watch—that the great idea surged into my brain. At four minutes to twelve I had been grumbling impotently at Providence. By two minutes to twelve I had determined upon a manly and independent course of action.

Briefly it was this. Providence had failed to give satisfaction. I would, therefore, cease any connection with it, and start a rival business on my own account. After all, if you want a thing done well, you must do it yourself.

In other words, since a dramatic accident and rescue would not happen of its own accord, I would arrange one for myself. Hawk looked to me the sort of man who would do anything in a friendly way for a few shillings.

I had now to fight it out with Conscience. I quote the brief report which subsequently appeared in the *Recording Angel*:—

THREE-ROUND CONTEST: CONSCIENCE (CELESTIAL B.C.)
v. J. GARNET (UNATTACHED).

Round One.—Conscience came to the scratch smiling and confident. Led off lightly with a statement that it would be bad for a man of the professor's age to get wet. Garnet countered heavily, alluding to the warmth of the weather and the fact that the professor habitually enjoyed a bathe every day. Much sparring, Conscience not quite so confident, and apparently afraid to come to close quarters with this man. Time called, with little damage done.

Round Two.—Conscience, much freshened by the half minute's rest, feinted with the charge of deceitfulness, and nearly got home heavily with "What would Phyllis say if she knew?" Garnet, however, side-stepped cleverly with "But she won't know," and followed up the advantage with a damaging, "Besides, it's all for the best." The round ended with a brisk rally on general principles, Garnet crowding in a lot of work. Conscience down twice, and only saved by the call of time.

Round Three (and last).—Conscience came up very weak, and with Garnet as strong as ever it was plain that the round would be a brief one. This proved to be the case. Early in the second minute Garnet cross-countered with "All's Fair in Love and War." Conscience down and out. The winner left the ring without a mark.

I rose, feeling much refreshed.

That afternoon I interviewed Mr. Hawk in the bar-parlour of the Net and Mackerel.

"Hawk," I said to him darkly, over a mystic and conspirator-like pot of ale, "I want you, next time you take Professor Derrick out fishing"—here I glanced round, to make sure that we were not overheard—"to upset him."

His astonished face rose slowly from the pot of ale like a full moon.

"What 'ud I do that for?" he gasped.

"Five shillings, I hope," said I, "but I am prepared to go to ten."

He gurgled.

I encored his pot of ale.

He kept on gurgling.

I argued with the man.

I spoke splendidly. I was eloquent, but at the same time concise. My choice of words was superb. I crystallised my ideas into pithy sentences which a child could have understood.

And at the end of half-an-hour he had grasped the salient points of the scheme. Also he imagined that I wished the professor upset by way of a practical joke. He gave me to understand that this was the type of humour which was to be expected from a gentleman from London. I am afraid he must at one period in his career have lived at one of those watering-places at which trippers congregate. He did not seem to think highly of the Londoner.

I let it rest at that. I could not give my true reason, and this served as well as any.

AT THE LAST MOMENT HE recollected that he, too, would get wet when the accident took place, and he raised the price to a sovereign.

A mercenary man. It is painful to see how rapidly the old simple spirit is dying out of our rural districts. Twenty years ago a fisherman would have been charmed to do a little job like that for a screw of tobacco.

XI

The Brave Preserver

I could have wished, during the next few days, that Mr. Harry Hawk's attitude towards myself had not been so unctuously confidential and mysterious. It was unnecessary, in my opinion, for him to grin meaningly when he met me in the street. His sly wink when we passed each other on the Cob struck me as in indifferent taste. The thing had been definitely arranged (ten shillings down and ten when it was over), and there was no need for any cloak and dark-lantern effects. I objected strongly to being treated as the villain of a melodrama. I was merely an ordinary well-meaning man, forced by circumstances into doing the work of Providence. Mr. Hawk's demeanour seemed to say, "We are two reckless scoundrels, but bless you, *I* won't give away your guilty secret." The climax came one morning as I was going along the street towards the beach. I was passing a dark doorway, when out shimmered Mr. Hawk as if he had been a spectre instead of the most substantial man within a radius of ten miles.

"'St!" He whispered.

"Now look here, Hawk," I said wrathfully, for the start he had given me had made me bite my tongue, "this has got to stop. I refuse to be haunted in this way. What is it now?"

"Mr. Derrick goes out this morning, zur."

"Thank goodness for that," I said. "Get it over this morning, then, without fail. I couldn't stand another day of it."

I went on to the Cob, where I sat down. I was excited. Deeds of great import must shortly be done. I felt a little nervous. It would never do to bungle the thing. Suppose by some accident I were to drown the professor! Or suppose that, after all, he contented himself with a mere formal expression of thanks, and refused to let bygones be bygones. These things did not bear thinking of.

I got up and began to pace restlessly to and fro.

Presently from the farther end of the harbour there put off Mr. Hawk's boat, bearing its precious cargo. My mouth became dry with excitement.

Very slowly Mr. Hawk pulled round the end of the Cob, coming to a standstill some dozen yards from where I was performing my beat. It was evidently here that the scene of the gallant rescue had been fixed.

My eyes were glued upon Mr. Hawk's broad back. Only when going in to bat at cricket have I experienced a similar feeling of suspense. The boat lay almost motionless on the water. I had never seen the sea smoother. Little ripples plashed against the side of the Cob.

It seemed as if this perfect calm might continue for ever. Mr. Hawk made no movement. Then suddenly the whole scene changed to one of vast activity. I heard Mr. Hawk utter a hoarse cry, and saw him plunge violently in his seat. The professor turned half round, and I caught sight of his indignant face, pink with emotion. Then the scene changed again with the rapidity of a dissolving view. I saw Mr. Hawk give another plunge, and the next moment the boat was upside down in the water, and I was shooting headforemost to the bottom, oppressed with the indescribably clammy sensation which comes when one's clothes are thoroughly wet.

I rose to the surface close to the upturned boat. The first sight I saw was the spluttering face of Mr. Hawk. I ignored him, and swam to where the professor's head bobbed on the waters.

"Keep cool," I said. A silly remark in the circumstances.

He was swimming energetically but unskilfully. He appeared to be one of those men who can look after themselves in the water only when they are in bathing costume. In his shore clothes it would have taken him a week to struggle to land, if he had got there at all, which was unlikely.

I know all about saving people from drowning. We used to practise it with a dummy in the swimming-bath at school. I attacked him from the rear, and got a good grip of him by the shoulders. I then swam on my back in the direction of land, and beached him with much *eclat* at the feet of an admiring crowd. I had thought of putting him under once or twice just to show him he was being rescued, but decided against such a course as needlessly realistic. As it was, I fancy he had swallowed of sea-water two or three hearty draughts.

The crowd was enthusiastic.

"Brave young feller," said somebody.

I blushed. This was Fame.

"Jumped in, he did, sure enough, an' saved the gentleman!"

"Be the old soul drownded?"

"That girt fule, 'Arry 'Awk!"

I was sorry for Mr. Hawk. Popular opinion was against him. What the professor said of him, when he recovered his breath, I cannot repeat,—not because I do not remember it, but because there is a line, and one must draw it. Let it be sufficient to say that on the subject of Mr. Hawk he saw eye to eye with the citizen who had described him as a "girt fule." I could not help thinking that my fellow conspirator did well to keep out of it all. He was now sitting in the boat, which he had restored to its normal position, baling pensively with an old tin can. To satire from the shore he paid no attention.

The professor stood up, and stretched out his hand. I grasped it.

"Mr. Garnet," he said, for all the world as if he had been the father of the heroine of "Hilda's Hero," "we parted recently in anger. Let me thank you for your gallant conduct and hope that bygones will be bygones."

I came out strong. I continued to hold his hand. The crowd raised a sympathetic cheer.

I said, "Professor, the fault was mine. Show that you have forgiven me by coming up to the farm and putting on something dry."

"An excellent idea, me boy; I *am* a little wet."

"A little," I agreed.

We walked briskly up the hill to the farm.

Ukridge met us at the gate.

He diagnosed the situation rapidly.

"You're all wet," he said. I admitted it.

"Professor Derrick has had an unfortunate boating accident," I explained.

"And Mr. Garnet heroically dived in, in all his clothes, and saved me life," broke in the professor. "A hero, sir. A—*choo!*"

"You're catching cold, old horse," said Ukridge, all friendliness and concern, his little differences with the professor having vanished like thawed snow. "This'll never do. Come upstairs and get into something of Garnet's. My own toggery wouldn't fit. What? Come along, come along, I'll get you some hot water. Mrs. Beale—Mrs. *Beale*! We want a large can of hot water. At once. What? Yes, immediately. What? Very well then, as soon as you can. Now then, Garny, my boy, out with the duds. What do you think of this, now, professor? A sweetly pretty thing in grey flannel. Here's a shirt. Get out of that wet toggery, and Mrs. Beale shall dry it. Don't attempt to tell me about it till you're changed. Socks! Socks forward. Show socks. Here you are. Coat? Try this blazer. That's right—that's right."

He bustled about till the professor was clothed, then marched him downstairs, and gave him a cigar.

"Now, what's all this? What happened?"

The professor explained. He was severe in his narration upon the unlucky Mr. Hawk.

"I was fishing, Mr. Ukridge, with me back turned, when I felt the boat rock violently from one side to the other to such an extent that I nearly lost me equilibrium, and then the boat upset. The man's a fool, sir. I could not see what had happened, my back being turned, as I say."

"Garnet must have seen. What happened, old horse?"

"It was very sudden," I said. "It seemed to me as if the man had got an attack of cramp. That would account for it. He has the reputation of being a most sober and trustworthy fellow."

"Never trust that sort of man," said Ukridge. "They are always the worst. It's plain to me that this man was beastly drunk, and upset the boat while trying to do a dance."

"A great curse, drink," said the professor. "Why, yes, Mr. Ukridge, I think I will. Thank you. Thank you. That will be enough. Not all the soda, if you please. Ah! this tastes pleasanter than salt water, Mr. Garnet. Eh? Eh? Ha—Ha!"

He was in the best of tempers, and I worked strenuously to keep him so. My scheme had been so successful that its iniquity did not worry me. I have noticed that this is usually the case in matters of this kind. It is the bungled crime that brings remorse.

"We must go round the links together one of these days, Mr. Garnet," said the professor. "I have noticed you there on several occasions, playing a strong game. I have lately taken to using a wooden putter. It is wonderful what a difference it makes."

Golf is a great bond of union. We wandered about the grounds discussing the game, the *entente cordiale* growing more firmly established every moment.

"We must certainly arrange a meeting," concluded the professor. "I shall be interested to see how we stand with regard to one another. I have improved my game considerably since I have been down here. Considerably."

"My only feat worthy of mention since I started the game," I said, "has been to halve a round with Angus M'Lurkin at St. Andrews."

"*The* M'Lurkin?" asked the professor, impressed.

"Yes. But it was one of his very off days, I fancy. He must have had gout or something. And I have certainly never played so well since."

"Still—," said the professor. "Yes, we must really arrange to meet."

With Ukridge, who was in one of his less tactless moods, he became very friendly.

Ukridge's ready agreement with his strictures on the erring Hawk had a great deal to do with this. When a man has a grievance, he feels drawn to those who will hear him patiently and sympathise. Ukridge was all sympathy.

"The man is an unprincipled scoundrel," he said, "and should be torn limb from limb. Take my advice, and don't go out with him again. Show him that you are not a man to be trifled with. The spilt child dreads the water, what? Human life isn't safe with such men as Hawk roaming about."

"You are perfectly right, sir. The man can have no defence. I shall not employ him again."

I felt more than a little guilty while listening to this duet on the subject of the man whom I had lured from the straight and narrow path. But the professor would listen to no defence. My attempts at excusing him were ill received. Indeed, the professor shewed such signs of becoming heated that I abandoned my fellow-conspirator to his fate with extreme promptness. After all, an addition to the stipulated reward—one of these days—would compensate him for any loss which he might sustain from the withdrawal of the professor's custom. Mr. Harry Hawk was in good enough case. I would see that he did not suffer.

Filled with these philanthropic feelings, I turned once more to talk with the professor of niblicks and approach shots and holes done in three without a brassy. We were a merry party at lunch—a lunch fortunately in Mrs. Beale's best vein, consisting of a roast chicken and sweets. Chicken had figured somewhat frequently of late on our daily bill of fare.

We saw the professor off the premises in his dried clothes, and I turned back to put the fowls to bed in a happier frame of mind than I had known for a long time. I whistled rag-time airs as I worked.

"Rum old buffer," said Ukridge meditatively, pouring himself out another whisky and soda. "My goodness, I should have liked to have seen him in the water. Why do I miss these good things?"

XII

Some Emotions and Yellow Lupin

T he fame which came to me through that gallant rescue was a little embarrassing. I was a marked man. Did I walk through the village, heads emerged from windows, and eyes followed me out of sight. Did I sit on the beach, groups formed behind me and watched in silent admiration. I was the man of the moment.

"If we'd wanted an advertisement for the farm," said Ukridge on one of these occasions, "we couldn't have had a better one than you, Garny, my boy. You have brought us three distinct orders for eggs during the last week. And I'll tell you what it is, we need all the orders we can get that'll bring us in ready money. The farm is in a critical condition. The coffers are low, deuced low. And I'll tell you another thing. I'm getting precious tired of living on nothing but chicken and eggs. So's Millie, though she doesn't say so."

"So am I," I said, "and I don't feel like imitating your wife's proud reserve. I never want to see a chicken again. As for eggs, they are far too much for us."

For the last week monotony had been the keynote of our commissariat. We had had cold chicken and eggs for breakfast, boiled chicken and eggs for lunch, and roast chicken and eggs for dinner. Meals became a nuisance, and Mrs. Beale complained bitterly that we did not give her a chance. She was a cook who would have graced an alderman's house and served up noble dinners for gourmets, and here she was in this remote corner of the world ringing the changes on boiled chicken and roast chicken and boiled eggs and poached eggs. Mr. Whistler, set to paint sign-boards for public-houses, might have felt the same restless discontent. As for her husband, the Hired Retainer, he took life as tranquilly as ever, and seemed to regard the whole thing as the most exhilarating farce he had ever been in. I think he looked on Ukridge as an amiable lunatic, and was content to rough it a little in order to enjoy the privilege of observing his movements. He made no complaints of the food. When a man has supported life for a number of years on incessant Army beef, the monotony of daily chicken and eggs scarcely strikes him.

"The fact is," said Ukridge, "these tradesmen round here seem to be a sordid, suspicious lot. They clamour for money."

He mentioned a few examples. Vickers, the butcher, had been the first to strike, with the remark that he would like to see the colour of Mr. Ukridge's money before supplying further joints. Dawlish, the grocer, had expressed almost exactly similar sentiments two days later; and the ranks of these passive resisters had been receiving fresh recruits ever since. To a man the tradesmen of Combe Regis seemed as deficient in Simple Faith as they were in Norman Blood.

"Can't you pay some of them a little on account?" I suggested. "It would set them going again."

"My dear old man," said Ukridge impressively, "we need every penny of ready money we can raise for the farm. The place simply eats money. That infernal roop let us in for I don't know what."

That insidious epidemic had indeed proved costly. We had painted the throats of the chickens with the best turpentine—at least Ukridge and Beale had,—but in spite of their efforts, dozens had died, and we had been obliged to sink much more money than was pleasant in restocking the run. The battle which took place on the first day after the election of the new members was a sight to remember. The results of it were still noticeable in the depressed aspect of certain of the recently enrolled.

"No," said Ukridge, summing up, "these men must wait. We can't help their troubles. Why, good gracious, it isn't as if they'd been waiting for the money long. We've not been down here much over a month. I never heard of such a scandalous thing. 'Pon my word, I've a good mind to go round, and have a straight talk with one or two of them. I come and settle down here, and stimulate trade, and give them large orders, and they worry me with bills when they know I'm up to my eyes in work, looking after the fowls. One can't attend to everything. The business is just now at its most crucial point. It would be fatal to pay any attention to anything else with things as they are. These scoundrels will get paid all in good time."

It is a peculiarity of situations of this kind that the ideas of debtor and creditor as to what constitutes a good time never coincide.

I AM AFRAID THAT, DESPITE the urgent need for strict attention to business, I was inclined to neglect my duties about this time. I had got into the habit of wandering off, either to the links, where I generally found the professor, sometimes Phyllis, or on long walks by myself. There was one particular walk along the cliffs, through some of the most beautiful scenery I have ever set eyes on, which more than any other suited my mood. I would work my way through the woods till I came to a small clearing on the very edge of the cliff. There I would sit and smoke by the hour. If ever I am stricken with smoker's heart, or staggers, or tobacco amblyopia, or any other of the cheery things which doctors predict for the devotee of the weed, I shall feel that I sowed the seeds of it that summer in that little clearing overlooking the sea. A man in love needs much tobacco. A man thinking out a novel needs much tobacco. I was in the grip of both maladies. Somehow I found that my ideas flowed more readily in that spot than in any other.

I had not been inside the professor's grounds since the occasion when I had gone in through the box-wood hedge. But on the afternoon following my financial conversation with Ukridge I made my way thither, after a toilet which, from its length, should have produced better results than it did. Not for four whole days had I caught so much as a glimpse of Phyllis. I had been to the links three times, and had met the professor twice, but on both occasions she had been absent. I had not had the courage to ask after her. I had an absurd idea that my voice or my manner would betray me in some way. I felt that I should have put the question with such an exaggerated show of indifference that all would have been discovered.

The professor was not at home. Nor was Mr. Chase. Nor was Miss Norah Derrick, the lady I had met on the beach with the professor. Miss Phyllis, said the maid, was in the garden.

I went into the garden. She was sitting under the cedar by the tennis-lawn, reading. She looked up as I approached.

I said it was a lovely afternoon. After which there was a lull in the conversation. I was filled with a horrid fear that I was boring her. I had probably arrived at the very moment when she was most interested in her book. She must, I thought, even now be regarding me as a nuisance, and was probably rehearsing bitter things to say to the maid for not having had the sense to explain that she was out.

"I—er—called in the hope of seeing Professor Derrick," I said.

"You would find him on the links," she replied. It seemed to me that she spoke wistfully.

"Oh, it—it doesn't matter," I said. "It wasn't anything important."

This was true. If the professor had appeared then and there, I should have found it difficult to think of anything to say to him which would have accounted to any extent for my anxiety to see him.

"How are the chickens, Mr. Garnet?" said she.

The situation was saved. Conversationally, I am like a clockwork toy. I have to be set going. On the affairs of the farm I could speak fluently. I sketched for her the progress we had made since her visit. I was humorous concerning roop, epigrammatic on the subject of the Hired Retainer and Edwin.

"Then the cat did come down from the chimney?" said Phyllis.

We both laughed, and—I can answer for myself—I felt the better for it.

"He came down next day," I said, "and made an excellent lunch of one of our best fowls. He also killed another, and only just escaped death himself at the hands of Ukridge."

"Mr. Ukridge doesn't like him, does he?"

"If he does, he dissembles his love. Edwin is Mrs. Ukridge's pet. He is the only subject on which they disagree. Edwin is certainly in the way on a chicken farm. He has got over his fear of Bob, and is now perfectly lawless. We have to keep a steady eye on him."

"And have you had any success with the incubator? I love incubators. I have always wanted to have one of my own, but we have never kept fowls."

"The incubator has not done all that it should have done," I said. "Ukridge looks after it, and I fancy his methods are not the right methods. I don't know if I have got the figures absolutely correct, but Ukridge reasons on these lines. He says you are supposed to keep the temperature up to a hundred and five degrees. I think he said a hundred and five. Then the eggs are supposed to hatch out in a week or so. He argues that you may just as well keep the temperature at seventy-two, and wait a fortnight for your chickens. I am certain there's a fallacy in the system somewhere, because we never seem to get as far as the chickens. But Ukridge says his theory is mathematically sound, and he sticks to it."

"Are you quite sure that the way you are doing it is the best way to manage a chicken farm?"

"I should very much doubt it. I am a child in these matters. I had only seen a chicken in its wild state once or twice before we came down here. I had never dreamed of being an active assistant on a real farm. The whole thing began like Mr. George Ade's fable of the Author. An Author—myself—was sitting at his desk trying to turn out any old thing that could be converted into breakfast-food when a friend came in and sat down on the table, and told him to go right on and not mind him."

"Did Mr. Ukridge do that?"

"Very nearly that. He called at my rooms one beautiful morning when I was feeling desperately tired of London and overworked and dying for a holiday, and suggested that I should come to Combe Regis with him and help him farm chickens. I have not regretted it."

"It is a lovely place, isn't it?"

"The loveliest I have ever seen. How charming your garden is."

"Shall we go and look at it? You have not seen the whole of it."

As she rose, I saw her book, which she had laid face downwards on the grass beside her. It was the same much-enduring copy of the "Manoeuvres of Arthur." I was thrilled. This patient perseverance must surely mean something. She saw me looking at it.

"Did you draw Pamela from anybody?" she asked suddenly.

I was glad now that I had not done so. The wretched Pamela, once my pride, was for some reason unpopular with the only critic about whose opinion I cared, and had fallen accordingly from her pedestal.

As we wandered down from the garden paths, she gave me her opinion of the book. In the main it was appreciative. I shall always associate the scent of yellow lupin with the higher criticism.

"Of course, I don't know anything about writing books," she said.

"Yes?" my tone implied, or I hope it did, that she was an expert on books, and that if she was not it didn't matter.

"But I don't think you do your heroines well. I have just got 'The Outsider—'" (My other novel. Bastable & Kirby, 6s. Satirical. All about Society—of which I know less than I know about chicken-farming. Slated by *Times* and *Spectator*. Well received by *London Mail* and *Winning Post*)—"and," continued Phyllis, "Lady Maud is exactly the same as Pamela in the 'Manoeuvres of Arthur.' I thought you must have drawn both characters from some one you knew."

"No," I said. "No. Purely imaginary."

"I am so glad," said Phyllis.

And then neither of us seemed to have anything to say. My knees began to tremble. I realised that the moment had arrived when my fate must be put to the touch; and I feared that the moment was premature. We cannot arrange these things to suit ourselves. I knew that the time was not yet ripe; but the magic scent of the yellow lupin was too much for me.

"Miss Derrick," I said hoarsely.

Phyllis was looking with more intentness than the attractions of the flower justified at a rose she held in her hand. The bee hummed in the lupin.

"Miss Derrick," I said, and stopped again.

"I say, you people," said a cheerful voice, "tea is ready. Hullo, Garnet, how are you? That medal arrived yet from the Humane Society?"

I spun round. Mr. Tom Chase was standing at the end of the path. The only word that could deal adequately with the situation slapped against my front teeth. I grinned a sickly grin.

"Well, Tom," said Phyllis.

And there was, I thought, just the faintest tinkle of annoyance in her voice.

"I've been bathing," said Mr. Chase, *a propos des bottes*.

"Oh," I replied. "And I wish," I added, "that you'd drowned yourself."

But I added it silently to myself.

XIII

Tea and Tennis

M et the professor's late boatman on the Cob," said Mr. Chase, dissecting a chocolate cake.

"Clumsy man," said Phyllis. "I hope he was ashamed of himself. I shall never forgive him for trying to drown papa."

My heart bled for Mr. Henry Hawk, that modern martyr.

"When I met him," said Tom Chase, "he looked as if he had been trying to drown his sorrow as well."

"I knew he drank," said Phyllis severely, "the very first time I saw him."

"You might have warned the professor," murmured Mr. Chase.

"He couldn't have upset the boat if he had been sober."

"You never know. He may have done it on purpose."

"Tom, how absurd."

"Rather rough on the man, aren't you?" I said.

"Merely a suggestion," continued Mr. Chase airily. "I've been reading sensational novels lately, and it seems to me that Mr. Hawk's cut out to be a minion. Probably some secret foe of the professor's bribed him."

My heart stood still. Did he know, I wondered, and was this all a roundabout way of telling me he knew?

"The professor may be a member of an Anarchist League, or something, and this is his punishment for refusing to assassinate some sportsman."

"Have another cup of tea, Tom, and stop talking nonsense."

Mr. Chase handed in his cup.

"What gave me the idea that the upset was done on purpose was this. I saw the whole thing from the Ware Cliff. The spill looked to me just like dozens I had seen at Malta."

"Why do they upset themselves on purpose at Malta particularly?" inquired Phyllis.

"Listen carefully, my dear, and you'll know more about the ways of the Navy that guards your coasts than you did before. When men are allowed on shore at Malta, the owner has a fancy to see them snugly on board again at a certain reasonable hour. After that hour any Maltese policeman who brings them aboard gets one sovereign, cash. But he has to do all the bringing part of it on his own. Consequence is, you see boats rowing out to the ship, carrying men who have overstayed their leave; and when they get near enough, the able-bodied gentleman in custody jumps to his feet, upsets the boat, and swims for the gangway. The policemen, if they aren't drowned—they sometimes are—race him, and whichever gets there first wins. If it's the policeman, he gets his sovereign. If it's the sailor, he is considered to have arrived not in a state of custody and gets off easier. What a judicious remark that was of the governor of North Carolina to the governor of South Carolina, respecting the length of time between drinks. Just one more cup, please, Phyllis."

"But how does all that apply?" I asked, dry-mouthed.

"Mr. Hawk upset the professor just as those Maltese were upset. There's a patent way of doing it. Furthermore, by judicious questioning, I found that Hawk was once in the Navy, and stationed at Malta. *Now*, who's going to drag in Sherlock Holmes?"

"You don't really think—?" I said, feeling like a criminal in the dock when the case is going against him.

"I think friend Hawk has been re-enacting the joys of his vanished youth, so to speak."

"He ought to be prosecuted," said Phyllis, blazing with indignation.

Alas, poor Hawk!

"Nobody's safe with a man of that sort, hiring out a boat." Oh, miserable Hawk!

"But why on earth should he play a trick like that on Professor Derrick, Chase?"

"Pure animal spirits, probably. Or he may, as I say, be a minion."

I was hot all over.

"I shall tell father that," said Phyllis in her most decided voice, "and see what he says. I don't wonder at the man taking to drink after doing such a thing."

"I—I think you're making a mistake," I said.

"I never make mistakes," Mr. Chase replied. "I am called Archibald the All-Right, for I am infallible. I propose to keep a reflective eye upon the jovial Hawk."

He helped himself to another section of the chocolate cake.

"Haven't you finished *yet*, Tom?" inquired Phyllis. "I'm sure Mr. Garnet's getting tired of sitting talking here," she said.

I shot out a polite negative. Mr. Chase explained with his mouth full that he had by no means finished. Chocolate cake, it appeared, was the dream of his life. When at sea he was accustomed to lie awake o' nights thinking of it.

"You don't seem to realise," he said, "that I have just come from a cruise on a torpedo-boat. There was such a sea on as a rule that cooking operations were entirely suspended, and we lived on ham and sardines—without bread."

"How horrible!"

"On the other hand," added Mr. Chase philosophically, "it didn't matter much, because we were all ill most of the time."

"Don't be nasty, Tom."

"I was merely defending myself. I hope Mr. Hawk will be able to do as well when his turn comes. My aim, my dear Phyllis, is to show you in a series of impressionist pictures the sort of thing I have to go through when I'm not here. Then perhaps you won't rend me so savagely over a matter of five minutes' lateness for breakfast."

"Five minutes! It was three-quarters of an hour, and everything was simply frozen."

"Quite right too in weather like this. You're a slave to convention, Phyllis. You think breakfast ought to be hot, so you always have it hot. On occasion I prefer mine cold. Mine is the truer wisdom. You can give the cook my compliments, Phyllis, and tell her—gently, for I don't wish the glad news to overwhelm her—that I enjoyed that cake. Say that I shall be glad to hear from her again. Care for a game of tennis, Garnet?"

"What a pity Norah isn't here," said Phyllis. "We could have had a four."

"But she is at present wasting her sweetness on the desert air of Yeovil. You had better sit down and watch us, Phyllis. Tennis in this sort of weather is no job for the delicately-nurtured feminine. I will explain the finer points of my play as we go on. Look out particularly for the Tilden Back-Handed Slosh. A winner every time."

We proceeded to the tennis court. I played with the sun in my eyes. I might, if I chose, emphasise that fact, and attribute my subsequent rout to it, adding, by way of solidifying the excuse, that I was playing in a strange court with a borrowed racquet, and that my mind was preoccupied—firstly, with *l'affaire* Hawk, secondly, and chiefly, with the gloomy thought that Phyllis and my opponent seemed to be on friendly terms with each other. Their manner at tea had been almost that of an engaged couple. There was a thorough understanding between them. I will not, however, take refuge behind excuses. I admit, without qualifying the statement, that Mr. Chase was too good for me. I had always been under the impression that lieutenants in the Royal Navy were not brilliant at tennis. I had met them at various houses, but they had never shone conspicuously. They had played an earnest, unobtrusive game, and generally seemed glad when it was over. Mr. Chase was not of this sort. His service was bottled lightning. His returns behaved like jumping crackers. He won the first game in precisely six strokes. He served. Only once did I take the service with the full face of the racquet, and then I seemed to be stopping a bullet. I returned it into the net. The last of the series struck the wooden edge of my racquet, and soared over the back net into the shrubbery, after the manner of a snick to long slip off a fast bowler.

"Game," said Mr. Chase, "we'll look for that afterwards."

I felt a worm and no man. Phyllis, I thought, would probably judge my entire character from this exhibition. A man, she would reflect, who could be so feeble and miserable a failure at tennis, could not be good for much in any department of life. She would compare me instinctively with my opponent, and contrast his dash and brilliance with my own inefficiency. Somehow the massacre was beginning to have a bad effect on my character. All my self-respect was ebbing. A little more of this, and I should become crushed,—a mere human jelly. It was my turn to serve. Service is my strong point at tennis. I am inaccurate, but vigorous, and occasionally send in a quite unplayable shot. One or two of these, even at the expense of a fault or so, and I might be permitted to retain at least a portion of my self-respect.

I opened with a couple of faults. The sight of Phyllis, sitting calm and cool in her chair under the cedar, unnerved me. I served another fault. And yet another.

"Here, I say, Garnet," observed Mr. Chase plaintively, "do put me out of this hideous suspense. I'm becoming a mere bundle of quivering ganglions."

I loathe facetiousness in moments of stress.

I frowned austerely, made no reply, and served another fault, my fifth.

Matters had reached a crisis. Even if I had to lob it underhand, I must send the ball over the net with the next stroke.

I restrained myself this time, eschewing the careless vigour which had marked my previous efforts. The ball flew in a slow semicircle, and pitched inside the correct court. At least, I told myself, I had not served a fault.

What happened then I cannot exactly say. I saw my opponent spring forward like a panther and whirl his racquet. The next moment the back net was shaking violently, and the ball was rolling swiftly along the ground on a return journey to the other court.

"Love-forty," said Mr. Chase. "Phyllis!"

"Yes?"

"That was the Tilden Slosh."

"I thought it must be," said Phyllis.

In the third game I managed to score fifteen. By the merest chance I returned one of his red-hot serves, and—probably through surprise— he failed to send it back again.

In the fourth and fifth games I omitted to score. Phyllis had left the cedar now, and was picking flowers from the beds behind the court.

We began the sixth game. And now for some reason I played really well. I struck a little vein of brilliance. I was serving, and this time a proportion of my serves went over the net instead of trying to get through. The score went from fifteen all to forty-fifteen. Hope began to surge through my veins. If I could keep this up, I might win yet.

The Tilden Slosh diminished my lead by fifteen. Then I got in a really fine serve, which beat him. 'Vantage In. Another Slosh. Deuce. Another Slam. 'Vantage out. It was an awesome moment. There is a tide in the affairs of men, which, taken by the flood—I served. Fault. I served again,—a beauty. He returned it like a flash into the corner of the court. With a supreme effort I got to it. We rallied. I was playing like a professor. Then whizz—!

The Slosh had beaten me on the post.

"Game *and*—," said Mr. Chase, tossing his racquet into the air and catching it by the handle. "Good game that last one."

I turned to see what Phyllis thought of it.

At the eleventh hour I had shown her of what stuff I was made.

She had disappeared.

"Looking for Miss Derrick?" said Chase, jumping the net, and joining me in my court, "she's gone into the house."

"When did she go?"

"At the end of the fifth game," said Chase.

"Gone to dress for dinner, I suppose," he continued. "It must be getting late. I think I ought to be going, too, if you don't mind. The professor gets a little restive if I keep him waiting for his daily bread. Great Scott, that watch can't be right! What do you make of it? Yes, so do I. I really think I must run. You won't mind. Good-night, then. See you tomorrow, I hope."

I walked slowly out across the fields. That same star, in which I had confided on a former occasion, was at its post. It looked placid and cheerful. *It* never got beaten by six games to love under the very eyes of a lady-star. *It* was never cut out ignominiously by infernally capable lieutenants in His Majesty's Navy. No wonder it was cheerful.

XIV

A Council of War

T he fact is," said Ukridge, "if things go on as they are now, my lad, we shall be in the cart. This business wants bucking up. We don't seem to be making headway. Why it is, I don't know, but we are *not* making headway. Of course, what we want is time. If only these scoundrels of tradesmen would leave us alone for a spell we could get things going properly. But we're hampered and rattled and worried all the time. Aren't we, Millie?"

"Yes, dear."

"You don't let me see the financial side of the thing enough," I complained. "Why don't you keep me thoroughly posted? I didn't know we were in such a bad way. The fowls look fit enough, and Edwin hasn't had one for a week."

"Edwin knows as well as possible when he's done wrong, Mr. Garnet," said Mrs. Ukridge. "He was so sorry after he had killed those other two."

"Yes," said Ukridge, "I saw to that."

"As far as I can see," I continued, "we're going strong. Chicken for breakfast, lunch, and dinner is a shade monotonous, perhaps, but look at the business we're doing. We sold a whole heap of eggs last week."

"But not enough, Garny old man. We aren't making our presence felt. England isn't ringing with our name. We sell a dozen eggs where we ought to be selling them by the hundred, carting them off in trucks for the London market and congesting the traffic. Harrod's and Whiteley's and the rest of them are beginning to get on their hind legs and talk. That's what they're doing. Devilish unpleasant they're making themselves. You see, laddie, there's no denying it—we *did* touch them for the deuce of a lot of things on account, and they agreed to take it out in eggs. All they've done so far is to take it out in apologetic letters from Millie. Now, I don't suppose there's a woman alive who can write a better apologetic letter than her nibs, but, if you're broad-minded and can face facts, you can't help seeing that the juiciest apologetic letter is not an egg. I meant to say, look at it from their point of view. Harrod—or Whiteley—comes into his store in the morning, rubbing his hands expectantly. 'Well,' he says, 'how many eggs from Combe Regis today?'

And instead of leading him off to a corner piled up with bursting crates, they show him a four-page letter telling him it'll all come right in the future. I've never run a store myself, but I should think that would jar a chap. Anyhow, the blighters seem to be getting tired of waiting."

"The last letter from Harrod's was quite pathetic," said Mrs. Ukridge sadly.

I had a vision of an eggless London. I seemed to see homes rendered desolate and lives embittered by the slump, and millionaires bidding against one another for the few rare specimens which Ukridge had actually managed to despatch to Brompton and Bayswater.

Ukridge, having induced himself to be broad-minded for five minutes, now began to slip back to his own personal point of view and became once more the man with a grievance. His fleeting sympathy with the wrongs of Mr. Harrod and Mr. Whiteley disappeared.

"What it all amounts to," he said complainingly, "is that they're infernally unreasonable. I've done everything possible to meet them. Nothing could have been more manly and straightforward than my attitude. I told them in my last letter but three that I proposed to let them have the eggs on the *Times* instalment system, and they said I was frivolous. They said that to send thirteen eggs as payment for goods supplied to the value of 25 pounds 1s. 8 1/2 d. was mere trifling. Trifling, I'll trouble you! That's the spirit in which they meet my suggestions. It was Harrod who did that. I've never met Harrod personally, but I'd like to, just to ask him if that's his idea of cementing amiable business relations. He knows just as well as anyone else that without credit commerce has no elasticity. It's an elementary rule. I'll bet he'd have been sick if chappies had refused to let him have tick when he was starting his store. Do you suppose Harrod, when he started in business, paid cash down on the nail for everything? Not a bit of it. He went about taking people by the coat-button and asking them to be good chaps and wait till Wednesday week. Trifling! Why, those thirteen eggs were absolutely all we had over after Mrs. Beale had taken what she wanted for the kitchen. As a matter of fact, if it's anybody's fault, it's Mrs. Beale's. That woman literally eats eggs."

"The habit is not confined to her," I said.

"Well, what I mean to say is, she seems to bathe in them."

"She says she needs so many for puddings, dear," said Mrs. Ukridge. "I spoke to her about it yesterday. And of course, we often have omelettes."

"She can't make omelettes without breaking eggs," I urged.

"She can't make them without breaking us, dammit," said Ukridge. "One or two more omelettes, and we're done for. No fortune on earth could stand it. We mustn't have any more omelettes, Millie. We must economise. Millions of people get on all right without omelettes. I suppose there are families where, if you suddenly produced an omelette, the whole strength of the company would get up and cheer, led by father. Cancel the omelettes, old girl, from now onward."

"Yes, dear. But—"

"Well?"

"I don't *think* Mrs. Beale would like that very much, dear. She has been complaining a good deal about chicken at every meal. She says that the omelettes are the only things that give her a chance. She says there are always possibilities in an omelette."

"In short," I said, "what you propose to do is deliberately to remove from this excellent lady's life the one remaining element of poetry. You mustn't do it. Give Mrs. Beale her omelettes, and let's hope for a larger supply of eggs."

"Another thing," said Ukridge. "It isn't only that there's a shortage of eggs. That wouldn't matter so much if only we kept hatching out fresh squads of chickens. I'm not saying the hens aren't doing their best. I take off my hat to the hens. As nice a hard-working lot as I ever want to meet, full of vigour and earnestness. It's that damned incubator that's letting us down all the time. The rotten thing won't work. *I* don't know what's the matter with it. The long and the short of it is that it simply declines to incubate."

"Perhaps it's your dodge of letting down the temperature. You remember, you were telling me? I forget the details."

"My dear old boy," he said earnestly, "there's nothing wrong with my figures. It's a mathematical certainty. What's the good of mathematics if not to help you work out that sort of thing? No, there's something deuced wrong with the machine itself, and I shall probably make a complaint to the people I got it from. Where did we get the incubator, old girl?"

"Harrod's, I think, dear,—yes, it was Harrod's. It came down with the first lot of things."

"Then," said Ukridge, banging the table with his fist, while his glasses flashed triumph, "we've got 'em. The Lord has delivered Harrod's into our hand. Write and answer that letter of theirs tonight, Millie. Sit on them."

"Yes, dear."

"Tell 'em that we'd have sent them their confounded eggs long ago, if only their rotten, twopenny-ha'penny incubator had worked with any approach to decency." He paused. "Or would you be sarcastic, Garny, old horse? No, better put it so that they'll understand. Say that I consider that the manufacturer of the thing ought to be in Colney Hatch—if he isn't there already—and that they are scoundrels for palming off a groggy machine of that sort on me."

"The ceremony of opening the morning's letters at Harrod's ought to be full of interest and excitement tomorrow," I said.

This dashing counter-stroke seemed to relieve Ukridge. His pessimism vanished. He seldom looked on the dark side of things for long at a time. He began now to speak hopefully of the future. He planned out ingenious improvements. Our fowls were to multiply so rapidly and consistently that within a short space of time Dorsetshire would be paved with them. Our eggs were to increase in size till they broke records and got three-line notices in the "Items of Interest" column in the *Daily Mail*. Briefly, each hen was to become a happy combination of rabbit and ostrich.

"There is certainly a good time coming," I said. "May it be soon. Meanwhile, what of the local tradesmen?"

Ukridge relapsed once more into gloom.

"They are the worst of the lot. I don't mind the London people so much. They only write, and a letter or two hurts nobody. But when it comes to butchers and bakers and grocers and fishmongers and fruiterers and what not coming up to one's house and dunning one in one's own garden,—well it's a little hard, what?"

"Oh, then those fellows I found you talking to yesterday were duns? I thought they were farmers, come to hear your views on the rearing of poultry."

"Which were they? Little chap with black whiskers and long, thin man with beard? That was Dawlish, the grocer, and Curtis, the fishmonger. The others had gone before you came."

It may be wondered why, before things came to such a crisis, I had not placed my balance at the bank at the disposal of the senior partner for use on behalf of the farm. The fact was that my balance was at the moment small. I have not yet in the course of this narrative gone into my pecuniary position, but I may state here that it was an inconvenient one. It was big with possibilities, but of ready cash there was but a meagre supply. My parents had been poor. But I had a wealthy uncle. Uncles are notoriously careless of the comfort of their nephews. Mine was no exception. He had views. He was a great believer in matrimony, as, having married three wives—not simultaneously—he had every right to be. He was also of opinion that the less money the young bachelor possessed, the better. The consequence was that he announced his intention of giving me a handsome allowance from the day that I married, but not an instant before. Till that glad day I would have to shift for myself. And I am bound to admit that—for an uncle—it was a remarkably sensible idea. I am also of the opinion that it is greatly to my credit, and a proof of my pure and unmercenary nature, that I did not instantly put myself up to be raffled for, or rush out into the streets and propose marriage to the first lady I met. But I was making quite enough with my pen to support myself, and, be it never so humble, there is something pleasant in a bachelor existence, or so I had thought until very recently.

I had thus no great stake in Ukridge's chicken farm. I had contributed a modest five pounds to the preliminary expenses, and another five after the roop incident. But further I could not go with safety. When his income is dependent on the whims of editors and publishers, the prudent man keeps something up his sleeve against a sudden slump in his particular wares. I did not wish to have to make a hurried choice between matrimony and the workhouse.

Having exhausted the subject of finance—or, rather, when I began to feel that it was exhausting me—I took my clubs, and strolled up the hill to the links to play off a match with a sportsman from the village. I had entered some days previously for a competition for a trophy (I quote the printed notice) presented by a local supporter of the game, in which up to the present I was getting on nicely. I had survived two rounds, and expected to beat my present opponent, which would bring me into the semi-final. Unless I had bad luck, I felt that I ought to get into the final, and win it. As far as I could gather from watching the play of my rivals, the professor was the best of them, and I was convinced that I should have no difficulty with him. But he had the most extraordinary luck at golf, though he never admitted it. He also exercised quite an uncanny influence on his opponent. I have seen men put completely off their stroke by his good fortune.

I disposed of my man without difficulty. We parted a little coldly. He had decapitated his brassy on the occasion of his striking Dorsetshire instead of his ball, and he was slow in recovering from the complex emotions which such an episode induces.

In the club-house I met the professor, whose demeanour was a welcome contrast to that of my late opponent. The professor had just routed his opponent, and so won through to the semi-final. He was warm, but jubilant.

I congratulated him, and left the place.

Phyllis was waiting outside. She often went round the course with him.

"Good afternoon," I said. "Have you been round with the professor?"

"Yes. We must have been in front of you. Father won his match."

"So he was telling me. I was very glad to hear it."

"Did you win, Mr. Garnet?"

"Yes. Pretty easily. My opponent had bad luck all through. Bunkers seemed to have a magnetic attraction for him."

"So you and father are both in the semi-final? I hope you will play very badly."

"Thank you," I said.

"Yes, it does sound rude, doesn't it? But father has set his heart on winning this year. Do you know that he has played in the final round two years running now?"

"Really?"

"Both times he was beaten by the same man."

"Who was that? Mr. Derrick plays a much better game than anybody I have seen on these links."

"It was nobody who is here now. It was a Colonel Jervis. He has not come to Combe Regis this year. That's why father is hopeful."

"Logically," I said, "he ought to be certain to win."

"Yes; but, you see, you were not playing last year, Mr. Garnet."

"Oh, the professor can make rings round me," I said.

"What did you go round in today?"

"We were playing match-play, and only did the first dozen holes; but my average round is somewhere in the late eighties."

"The best father has ever done is ninety, and that was only once. So you see, Mr. Garnet, there's going to be another tragedy this year."

"You make me feel a perfect brute. But it's more than likely, you must remember, that I shall fail miserably if I ever do play your father in the final. There are days when I play golf as badly as I play tennis. You'll hardly believe me."

She smiled reminiscently.

"Tom is much too good at tennis. His service is perfectly dreadful."

"It's a little terrifying on first acquaintance."

"But you're better at golf than at tennis, Mr. Garnet. I wish you were not."

"This is special pleading," I said. "It isn't fair to appeal to my better feelings, Miss Derrick."

"I didn't know golfers had any where golf was concerned. Do you really have your off-days?"

"Nearly always. There are days when I slice with my driver as if it were a bread-knife."

"Really?"

"And when I couldn't putt to hit a haystack."

"Then I hope it will be on one of those days that you play father."

"I hope so, too," I said.

"You hope so?"

"Yes."

"But don't you want to win?"

"I should prefer to please you."

"Really, how very unselfish of you, Mr. Garnet," she replied, with a laugh. "I had no idea that such chivalry existed. I thought a golfer would sacrifice anything to win a game."

"Most things."

"And trample on the feelings of anybody."

"Not everybody," I said.

At this point the professor joined us.

XV

The Arrival of Nemesis

S ome people do not believe in presentiments. They attribute that curious feeling that something unpleasant is going to happen to such mundane causes as liver, or a chill, or the weather. For my own part, I think there is more in the matter than the casual observer might imagine.

I awoke three days after my meeting with the professor at the club-house, filled with a dull foreboding. Somehow I seemed to know that that day was going to turn out badly for me. It may have been liver or a chill, but it was certainly not the weather. The morning was perfect,—the most glorious of a glorious summer. There was a haze over the valley and out to sea which suggested a warm noon, when the sun should have begun the serious duties of the day. The birds were singing in the trees and breakfasting on the lawn, while Edwin, seated on one of the flower-beds, watched them with the eye of a connoisseur. Occasionally, when a sparrow hopped in his direction, he would make a sudden spring, and the bird would fly away to the other side of the lawn. I had never seen Edwin catch a sparrow. I believe they looked on him as a bit of a crank, and humoured him by coming within springing distance, just to keep him amused. Dashing young cock-sparrows would show off before their particular hen-sparrows, and earn a cheap reputation for dare-devilry by going within so many years of Edwin's lair, and then darting away. Bob was in his favourite place on the gravel. I took him with me down to the Cob to watch me bathe.

"What's the matter with me today, Robert, old son?" I asked him, as I dried myself.

He blinked lazily, but contributed no suggestion.

"It's no good looking bored," I went on, "because I'm going to talk about myself, however much it bores you. Here am I, as fit as a prize-fighter, living in the open air for I don't know how long, eating good plain food—bathing every morning—sea-bathing, mind you—and yet what's the result? I feel beastly."

Bob yawned, and gave a little whine.

"Yes," I said, "I know I'm in love. But that can't be it, because I was in love just as much a week ago, and I felt all right then. But isn't she an angel, Bob? Eh? Isn't she? And didn't you feel bucked when she patted you? Of course you did. Anybody would. But how about Tom Chase? Don't you think he's a dangerous man? He calls her by her Christian name, you know, and behaves generally as if she belonged to him. And then he sees her every day, while I have to trust to meeting her at odd times, and then I generally feel such a fool I can't think of anything to talk about except golf and the weather. He probably sings duets with her after dinner, and you know what comes of duets after dinner."

Here Bob, who had been trying for some time to find a decent excuse for getting away, pretended to see something of importance at the other end of the Cob, and trotted off to investigate it, leaving me to finish dressing by myself.

"Of course," I said to myself, "It may be merely hunger. I may be all right after breakfast. But at present I seem to be working up for a really fine fit of the blues. I feel bad."

I whistled to Bob, and started for home. On the beach I saw the professor some little distance away, and waved my towel in a friendly manner. He made no reply.

Of course, it was possible that he had not seen me; but for some reason his attitude struck me as ominous. As far as I could see, he was looking straight at me, and he was not a short-sighted man. I could think of no reason why he should cut me. We had met on the links on the previous morning, and he had been friendliness itself. He had called me "me dear boy," supplied me with a gin and gingerbeer at the clubhouse, and generally behaved as if he had been David and I Jonathan. Yet in certain moods we are inclined to make mountains out of molehills, and I went on my way, puzzled and uneasy, with a distinct impression that I had received the cut direct.

I felt hurt. What had I done that Providence should make things so unpleasant for me? It would be a little hard, as Ukridge would have said, if, after all my trouble, the professor had discovered some fresh grievance against me. Perhaps Ukridge had been irritating him again. I wished he would not identify me so completely with Ukridge. I could not be expected to control the man. Then I reflected that they could hardly have met in the few hours between my parting from the professor at the club-house and my meeting with him on the beach. Ukridge rarely left the farm. When he was not working among the fowls, he was lying on his back in the paddock, resting his massive mind.

I came to the conclusion that after all the professor had not seen me.

"I'm an idiot, Bob," I said, as we turned in at the farm gate, "and I let my imagination run away with me."

Bob wagged his tail in approval of the sentiment.

Breakfast was ready when I got in. There was a cold chicken on the sideboard, devilled chicken on the table, a trio of boiled eggs, and a dish of scrambled eggs. As regarded quantity Mrs. Beale never failed us.

Ukridge was sorting the letters.

"Morning, Garny," he said. "One for you, Millie."

"It's from Aunt Elizabeth," said Mrs. Ukridge, looking at the envelope.

I had only heard casual mention of this relative hitherto, but I had built up a mental picture of her partly from remarks which Ukridge had let fall, but principally from the fact that he had named the most malignant hen in our fowl-run after her. A severe lady, I imagined with a cold eye.

"Wish she'd enclose a cheque," said Ukridge. "She could spare it. You've no idea, Garny, old man, how disgustingly and indecently rich that woman is. She lives in Kensington on an income which would do her well in Park Lane. But as a touching proposition she had proved almost negligible. She steadfastly refuses to part."

"I think she would, dear, if she knew how much we needed it. But I don't like to ask her. She's so curious, and says such horrid things."

"She does," agreed Ukridge, gloomily. He spoke as one who had had experience. "Two for you, Garny. All the rest for me. Ten of them, and all bills."

He spread the envelopes out on the table, and drew one at a venture.

"Whiteley's," he said. "Getting jumpy. Are in receipt of my favour of the 7th inst. and are at a loss to understand. It's rummy about these blighters, but they never seem able to understand a damn thing. It's hard! You put things in words of one syllable for them, and they just goggle and wonder what it all means. They want something on account. Upon my Sam, I'm disappointed with Whiteley's. I'd been thinking in rather a kindly spirit of them, and feeling that they were a more intelligent lot than Harrod's. I'd had half a mind to give Harrod's the miss-in-baulk and hand my whole trade over to these fellows. But not now, dash it! Whiteley's have disappointed me. From the way they write, you'd think they thought I was doing it for fun. How can I let them have their infernal money when there isn't any? Here's one from Dorchester. Smith, the chap we got the gramophone from. Wants to know when I'm going to settle up for sixteen records."

"Sordid brute!"

I wanted to get on with my own correspondence, but Ukridge held me with a glittering eye.

"The chicken-men, the dealer people, you know, want me to pay for the first lot of hens. Considering that they all died of roop, and that I was going to send them back anyhow after I'd got them to hatch out a few chickens, I call that cool. I mean to say, business is business. That's what these fellows don't seem to understand. I can't afford to pay enormous sums for birds which die off quicker than I can get them in."

"I shall never speak to Aunt Elizabeth again," said Mrs. Ukridge suddenly.

She had dropped the letter she had been reading, and was staring indignantly in front of her. There were two little red spots on her cheeks.

"What's the matter, old chap?" inquired Ukridge affectionately, glancing up from his pile of bills and forgetting his own troubles in an instant. "Buck up! Aunt Elizabeth been getting on your nerves again? What's she been saying this time?"

Mrs. Ukridge left the room with a sob. Ukridge sprang at the letter.

"If that demon doesn't stop writing her infernal letters and upsetting Millie, I shall strangle her with my bare hands, regardless of her age and sex." He turned over the pages of the letter till he came to the passage which had caused the trouble. "Well, upon my Sam! Listen to this, Garny, old horse. 'You tell me nothing regarding the success of this chicken farm of yours, and I confess that I find your silence ominous. You know my opinion of your husband. He is perfectly helpless in any matter requiring the exercise of a little common-sense and business capability.'" He stared at me, amazed. "I like that! 'Pon my soul, that is really rich! I could have believed almost anything of that blighted female, but I did think she had a reasonable amount of intelligence. Why, you know that it's just in matters requiring common-sense and business capability that I come out really strong."

"Of course, old man," I replied dutifully. "The woman's a fool."

"That's what she calls me two lines further on. No wonder Millie was upset. Why can't these cats leave people alone?"

"Oh, woman, woman!" I threw in helpfully.

"Always interfering—"

"Rotten!"

"And backbiting—"

"Awful!"

"I shan't stand it."

"I shouldn't!"

"Look here! On the next page she calls me a gaby!"

"It's time you took a strong line."

"And in the very next sentence refers to me as a perfect guffin. What's a guffin, Garny, old boy?"

I considered the point.

"Broadly speaking, I should say, one who guffs."

"I believe it's actionable."

"I shouldn't wonder."

Ukridge rushed to the door.

"Millie!"

He slammed the door, and I heard him dashing upstairs.

I turned to my letters. One was from Lickford, with a Cornish postmark. I glanced through it and laid it aside for a more exhaustive perusal.

The other was in a strange handwriting. I looked at the signature. "Patrick Derrick." This was queer. What had the professor to say to me?

The next moment my heart seemed to spring to my throat.

"Sir," the letter began.

A pleasant cheery opening!

Then it got off the mark, so to speak, like lightning. There was no sparring for an opening, no dignified parade of set phrases, leading up to the main point. It was the letter of a man who was almost too furious to write. It gave me the impression that, if he had not written it, he would have been obliged to have taken some very violent form of exercise by way of relief to his soul.

> "You will be good enough to look on our acquaintance as closed. I have no wish to associate with persons of your stamp. If we should happen to meet, you will be good enough to treat me as a total stranger, as I shall treat you. And, if I may be allowed to give you a word of advice, I should recommend you in future, when you wish to exercise your humour, to do so in some less practical manner than by bribing boatmen to upset your—(*friends* crossed out thickly, and *acquaintances* substituted.) If you require further enlightenment in this matter, the enclosed letter may be of service to you."

With which he remained mine faithfully, Patrick Derrick.

The enclosed letter was from one Jane Muspratt. It was bright and interesting.

DEAR SIR,

My Harry, Mr. Hawk, sas to me how it was him upsetting the boat and you, not because he is not steady in a boat which he is no man more so in Combe Regis, but because one of the gentlemen what keeps chikkens up the hill, the little one, Mr. Garnick his name is, says to him, Hawk, I'll give you a sovrin to upset Mr. Derick in your boat, and my Harry being esily led was took in and did, but he's sory now and wishes he hadn't, and he sas he'll niver do a prackticle joke again for anyone even for a banknote.

Yours obedly.,
JANE MUSPRATT

Oh, woman, woman!

At the bottom of everything! History is full of tragedies caused by the lethal sex. Who lost Mark Antony the world? A woman. Who let Samson in so atrociously? Woman again. Why did Bill Bailey leave home? Once more, because of a woman. And here was I, Jerry Garnet, harmless, well-meaning writer of minor novels, going through the same old mill.

I cursed Jane Muspratt. What chance had I with Phyllis now? Could I hope to win over the professor again? I cursed Jane Muspratt for the second time.

My thoughts wandered to Mr. Harry Hawk. The villain! The scoundrel! What business had he to betray me? . . . Well, I could settle with him. The man who lays a hand upon a woman, save in the way of kindness, is justly disliked by Society; so the woman Muspratt, culpable as she was, was safe from me. But what of the man Hawk? There no such considerations swayed me. I would interview the man Hawk. I would give him the most hectic ten minutes of his career. I would say things to him the recollection of which would make him start up shrieking in his bed in the small hours of the night. I would arise, and be a man, and slay him; take him grossly, full of bread, with all his crimes broad-blown, as flush as May, at gaming, swearing, or about some act that had no relish of salvation in it.

The Demon!

My life—ruined. My future—grey and black. My heart—shattered. And why? Because of the scoundrel, Hawk.

Phyllis would meet me in the village, on the Cob, on the links, and pass by as if I were the Invisible Man. And why? Because of the reptile, Hawk. The worm, Hawk. The dastard and varlet, Hawk.

I crammed my hat on, and hurried out of the house towards the village.

XVI

A Chance Meeting

I roamed the place in search of the varlet for the space of half-an-hour, and, after having drawn all his familiar haunts, found him at length leaning over the sea-wall near the church, gazing thoughtfully into the waters below.

I confronted him.

"Well," I said, "you're a beauty, aren't you?"

He eyed me owlishly. Even at this early hour, I was grieved to see, he showed signs of having looked on the bitter while it was brown. His eyes were filmy, and his manner aggressively solemn.

"Beauty?" he echoed.

"What have you got to say for yourself?"

"Say f'self."

It was plain that he was engaged in pulling his faculties together by some laborious process known only to himself. At present my words conveyed no meaning to him. He was trying to identify me. He had seen me before somewhere, he was certain, but he could not say where, or who I was.

"I want to know," I said, "what induced you to be such an abject idiot as to let our arrangement get known?"

I spoke quietly. I was not going to waste the choicer flowers of speech on a man who was incapable of understanding them. Later on, when he had awakened to a sense of his position, I would begin really to talk to him.

He continued to stare at me. Then a sudden flash of intelligence lit up his features.

"Mr. Garnick," he said at last.

"From ch—chicken farm," he continued, with the triumphant air of a cross-examining King's counsel who has at last got on the track.

"Yes," I said.

"Up top the hill," he proceeded, clinchingly. He stretched out a huge hand.

"How you?" he inquired with a friendly grin.

"I want to know," I said distinctly, "what you've got to say for yourself after letting our affair with the professor become public property?"

He paused awhile in thought.

"Dear sir," he said at last, as if he were dictating a letter, "dear sir, I owe you—ex—exp—"

He waved his hand, as who should say, "It's a stiff job, but I'm going to do it."

"Explashion," he said.

"You do," said I grimly. "I should like to hear it."

"Dear sir, listen me."

"Go on then."

"You came me. You said 'Hawk, Hawk, ol' fren', listen me. You tip this ol' bufflehead into watter,' you said, 'an' gormed if I don't give 'ee a poond note.' That's what you said me. Isn't that what you said me?"

I did not deny it.

"'Ve' well,' I said you. 'Right,' I said. I tipped the ol' soul into watter, and I got the poond note."

"Yes, you took care of that. All this is quite true, but it's beside the point. We are not disputing about what happened. What I want to know—for the third time—is what made you let the cat out of the bag? Why couldn't you keep quiet about it?"

He waved his hand.

"Dear sir," he replied, "this way. Listen me."

It was a tragic story that he unfolded. My wrath ebbed as I listened. After all the fellow was not so greatly to blame. I felt that in his place I should have acted as he had done. It was Fate's fault, and Fate's alone.

It appeared that he had not come well out of the matter of the accident. I had not looked at it hitherto from his point of view. While the rescue had left me the popular hero, it had had quite the opposite result for him. He had upset his boat and would have drowned his passenger, said public opinion, if the young hero from London—myself—had not plunged in, and at the risk of his life brought the professor ashore. Consequently, he was despised by all as an inefficient boatman. He became a laughing-stock. The local wags made laborious jests when he passed. They offered him fabulous sums to take their worst enemies out for a row with him. They wanted to know when he was going to school to learn his business. In fact, they behaved as wags do and always have done at all times all the world over.

Now, all this, it seemed, Mr. Hawk would have borne cheerfully and patiently for my sake, or, at any rate for the sake of the crisp pound note I had given him. But a fresh factor appeared in the problem, complicating it grievously. To wit, Miss Jane Muspratt.

"She said to me," explained Mr. Hawk with pathos, "'Harry 'Awk,' she said, 'yeou'm a girt fule, an' I don't marry noone as is ain't to be trusted in a boat by hisself, and what has jokes made about him by that Tom Leigh!'"

"I punched Tom Leigh," observed Mr. Hawk parenthetically. "'So,' she said me, 'you can go away, an' I don't want to see yeou again!'"

This heartless conduct on the part of Miss Muspratt had had the natural result of making him confess in self-defence; and she had written to the professor the same night.

I forgave Mr. Hawk. I think he was hardly sober enough to understand, for he betrayed no emotion. "It is Fate, Hawk," I said, "simply Fate. There is a Divinity that shapes our ends, rough-hew them how we will, and it's no good grumbling."

"Yiss," said Mr. Hawk, after chewing this sentiment for a while in silence, "so she said me, 'Hawk,' she said—like that—'you're a girt fule—'"

"That's all right," I replied. "I quite understand. As I say, it's simply Fate. Good-bye." And I left him.

As I was going back, I met the professor and Phyllis. They passed me without a look.

I wandered on in quite a fervour of self-pity. I was in one of those moods when life suddenly seems to become irksome, when the future stretches black and grey in front of one. I should have liked to have faded almost imperceptibly from the world, like Mr. Bardell, even if, as in his case, it had involved being knocked on the head with a pint pot in a public-house cellar.

In such a mood it is imperative that one should seek distraction. The shining example of Mr. Harry Hawk did not lure me. Taking to drink would be a nuisance. Work was what I wanted. I would toil like a navvy all day among the fowls, separating them when they fought, gathering in the eggs when they laid, chasing them across country when they got away, and even, if necessity arose, painting their throats with turpentine when they were stricken with roop. Then, after dinner, when the lamps were lit, and Mrs. Ukridge nursed Edwin and sewed, and Ukridge smoked cigars and incited the gramophone to murder "Mumbling Mose," I would steal away to my bedroom and write—and write—and *write*. And go on writing till my fingers were numb and my eyes refused to do their duty. And, when time had passed, I might come to feel that it was all for the best. A man must go through the fire before he can write his masterpiece. We learn in suffering what we teach in song. What we lose on the swings we make up on the roundabouts. Jerry Garnet, the Man, might become a depressed, hopeless wreck, with the iron planted immovably in his soul; but Jeremy Garnet, the Author, should turn out such a novel of gloom, that strong critics would weep, and the public jostle for copies till Mudie's doorway became a shambles.

Thus might I some day feel that all this anguish was really a blessing—effectively disguised.

But I doubted it.

We were none of us very cheerful now at the farm. Even Ukridge's spirit was a little daunted by the bills which poured in by every post. It was as if the tradesmen of the neighbourhood had formed a league, and were working in concert. Or it may have been due to thought-waves. Little accounts came not in single spies but in battalions. The popular demand for the sight of the colour of his money grew daily. Every morning at breakfast he would give us fresh bulletins of the state of mind of each of our creditors, and thrill us with the announcement that Whiteley's were getting cross, and Harrod's jumpy or that the bearings of Dawlish, the grocer, were becoming overheated. We lived in a continual atmosphere of worry. Chicken and nothing but chicken at meals, and chicken and nothing but chicken between meals had frayed our nerves. An air of defeat hung over the place. We were a beaten side, and we realised it. We had been playing an uphill game for nearly two months, and the strain was beginning to tell. Ukridge became uncannily silent. Mrs. Ukridge, though she did not understand, I fancy, the details of the matter, was worried because Ukridge was. Mrs. Beale had long since been turned into a soured cynic by the lack of chances vouchsafed her for the exercise of her art. And as for me, I have never since spent so profoundly miserably a week. I was not even permitted the anodyne of work. There seemed to be nothing to do on the farm. The chickens were quite happy, and only asked to be let alone and allowed to have their meals at regular intervals. And every day one or more of their number would vanish into the kitchen, Mrs. Beale would serve up the corpse in some cunning disguise, and we would try to delude ourselves into the idea that it was something altogether different.

There was one solitary gleam of variety in our menu. An editor sent me a cheque for a set of verses. We cashed that cheque and trooped round the town in a body, laying out the money. We bought a leg of mutton, and a tongue and sardines, and pine-apple chunks, and potted meat, and many other noble things, and had a perfect banquet. Mrs. Beale, with the scenario of a smile on her face, the first that she had worn in these days of stress, brought in the joint, and uncovered it with an air.

"Thank God!" said Ukridge, as he began to carve.

It was the first time I had ever heard him say a grace, and if ever an occasion merited such a deviation from habit, this occasion did.

After that we relapsed into routine again.

Deprived of physical labour, with the exception of golf and bathing— trivial sports compared with work in the fowl-run at its hardest—I tried to make up for it by working at my novel.

It refused to materialise.

The only progress I achieved was with my villain.

I drew him from the professor, and made him a blackmailer. He had several other social defects, but that was his profession. That was the thing he did really well.

It was on one of the many occasions on which I had sat in my room, pen in hand, through the whole of a lovely afternoon, with no better result than a slight headache, that I bethought me of that little paradise on the Ware Cliff, hung over the sea and backed by green woods. I had not been there for some time, owing principally to an entirely erroneous idea that I could do more solid work sitting in a straight hard chair at a table than lying on soft turf with the sea wind in my eyes.

But now the desire to visit that little clearing again drove me from my room. In the drawing-room below the gramophone was dealing brassily with "Mister Blackman." Outside the sun was just thinking of setting. The Ware Cliff was the best medicine for me. What does Kipling say?

> *"And soon you will find that the sun and the wind*
> *And the Djinn of the Garden, too,*
> *Have lightened the hump, Cameelious Hump,*
> *The Hump that is black and blue."*

His instructions include digging with a hoe and a shovel also, but I could omit that. The sun and the wind were what I needed.

I took the upper road. In certain moods I preferred it to the path along the cliff. I walked fast. The exercise was soothing.

To reach my favourite clearing I had to take to the fields on the left, and strike down hill in the direction of the sea. I hurried down the narrow path.

I broke into the clearing at a jog trot, and stood panting. And at the same moment, looking cool and beautiful in her white dress, Phyllis entered in from the other side. Phyllis—without the professor.

XVII

Of a Sentimental Nature

She was wearing a panama, and she carried a sketching-block and camp-stool.

"Good evening," I said.

"Good evening," said she.

It is curious how different the same words can sound, when spoken by different people. My "good evening" might have been that of a man with a particularly guilty conscience caught in the act of doing something more than usually ignoble. She spoke like a rather offended angel.

"It's a lovely evening," I went on pluckily.

"Very."

"The sunset!"

"Yes."

"Er—"

She raised a pair of blue eyes, devoid of all expression save a faint suggestion of surprise, and gazed through me for a moment at some object a couple of thousand miles away, and lowered them again, leaving me with a vague feeling that there was something wrong with my personal appearance.

Very calmly she moved to the edge of the cliff, arranged her camp-stool, and sat down. Neither of us spoke a word. I watched her while she filled a little mug with water from a little bottle, opened her paint-box, selected a brush, and placed her sketching-block in position.

She began to paint.

Now, by all the laws of good taste, I should before this have made a dignified exit. It was plain that I was not to be regarded as an essential ornament of this portion of the Ware Cliff. By now, if I had been the Perfect Gentleman, I ought to have been a quarter of a mile away.

But there is a definite limit to what a man can do. I remained.

The sinking sun flung a carpet of gold across the sea. Phyllis' hair was tinged with it. Little waves tumbled lazily on the beach below. Except for the song of a distant blackbird, running through its repertoire before retiring for the night, everything was silent.

She sat there, dipping and painting and dipping again, with never a word for me—standing patiently and humbly behind her.

"Miss Derrick," I said.

She half turned her head.

"Yes."

"Why won't you speak to me?" I said.

"I don't understand you."

"Why won't you speak to me?"

"I think you know, Mr. Garnet."

"It is because of that boat accident?"

"Accident!"

"Episode," I amended.

She went on painting in silence. From where I stood I could see her profile. Her chin was tilted. Her expression was determined.

"Is it?" I said.

"Need we discuss it?"

"Not if you do not wish it."

I paused.

"But," I added, "I should have liked a chance to defend myself. . . What glorious sunsets there have been these last few days. I believe we shall have this sort of weather for another month."

"I should not have thought that possible."

"The glass is going up," I said.

"I was not talking about the weather."

"It was dull of me to introduce such a worn-out topic."

"You said you could defend yourself."

"I said I should like the chance to do so."

"You have it."

"That's very kind of you. Thank you."

"Is there any reason for gratitude?"

"Every reason."

"Go on, Mr. Garnet. I can listen while I paint. But please sit down. I don't like being talked to from a height."

I sat down on the grass in front of her, feeling as I did so that the change of position in a manner clipped my wings. It is difficult to speak movingly while sitting on the ground. Instinctively I avoided eloquence. Standing up, I might have been pathetic and pleading. Sitting down, I was compelled to be matter-of-fact.

"You remember, of course, the night you and Professor Derrick dined with us? When I say dined, I use the word in a loose sense."

For a moment I thought she was going to smile. We were both

thinking of Edwin. But it was only for a moment, and then her face grew cold once more, and the chin resumed its angle of determination.

"Yes," she said.

"You remember the unfortunate ending of the festivities?"

"Well?"

"If you recall that at all clearly, you will also remember that the fault was not mine, but Ukridge's."

"Well?"

"It was his behaviour that annoyed Professor Derrick. The position, then, was this, that I was to be cut off from the pleasantest friendship I had ever formed—"

I stopped for a moment. She bent a little lower over her easel, but remained silent.

"—Simply through the tactlessness of a prize idiot."

"I like Mr. Ukridge."

"I like him, too. But I can't pretend that he is anything but an idiot at times."

"Well?"

"I naturally wished to mend matters. It occurred to me that an excellent way would be by doing your father a service. It was seeing him fishing that put the idea of a boat-accident into my head. I hoped for a genuine boat-accident. But those things only happen when one does not want them. So I determined to engineer one."

"You didn't think of the shock to my father."

"I did. It worried me very much."

"But you upset him all the same."

"Reluctantly."

She looked up, and our eyes met. I could detect no trace of forgiveness in hers.

"You behaved abominably," she said.

"I played a risky game, and I lost. And I shall now take the consequences. With luck I should have won. I did not have luck, and I am not going to grumble about it. But I am grateful to you for letting me explain. I should not have liked you to have gone on thinking that I played practical jokes on my friends. That is all I have to say. I think it was kind of you to listen. Good-bye, Miss Derrick."

I got up.

"Are you going?"

"Why not?"

"Please sit down again."

"But you wish to be alone—"

"Please sit down!"

There was a flush on the cheek turned towards me, and the chin was tilted higher.

I sat down.

To westward the sky had changed to the hue of a bruised cherry. The sun had sunk below the horizon, and the sea looked cold and leaden. The blackbird had long since flown.

"I am glad you told me, Mr. Garnet."

She dipped her brush in the water.

"Because I don't like to think badly of—people."

She bent her head over her painting.

"Though I still think you behaved very wrongly. And I am afraid my father will never forgive you for what you did."

Her father! As if he counted.

"But you do?" I said eagerly.

"I think you are less to blame than I thought you were at first."

"No more than that?"

"You can't expect to escape all consequences. You did a very stupid thing."

"I was tempted."

The sky was a dull grey now. It was growing dusk. The grass on which I sat was wet with dew.

I stood up.

"Isn't it getting a little dark for painting?" I said. "Are you sure you won't catch cold? It's very damp."

"Perhaps it is. And it is late, too."

She shut her paint-box, and emptied the little mug on to the grass.

"May I carry your things?" I said.

I think she hesitated, but only for a moment.

I possessed myself of the camp-stool, and we started on our homeward journey.

We were both silent. The spell of the quiet summer evening was on us.

"'And all the air a solemn stillness holds,'" she said softly. "I love this cliff, Mr. Garnet. It's the most soothing place in the world."

"I found it so this evening."

She glanced at me quickly.

"You're not looking well," she said. "Are you sure you are not overworking yourself?"

"No, it's not that."

Somehow we had stopped, as if by agreement, and were facing each other. There was a look in her eyes I had never seen there before. The twilight hung like a curtain between us and the world. We were alone together in a world of our own.

"It is because I had offended you," I said.

She laughed a high, unnatural laugh.

"I have loved you ever since I first saw you," I said doggedly.

XVIII

Ukridge Gives Me Advice

Hours after—or so it seemed to me—we reached the spot at which our ways divided. We stopped, and I felt as if I had been suddenly cast back into the workaday world from some distant and pleasanter planet. I think Phyllis must have felt much the same sensation, for we both became on the instant intensely practical and businesslike.

"But about your father," I said.

"That's the difficulty."

"He won't give us his consent?"

"I'm afraid he wouldn't dream of it."

"You can't persuade him?"

"I can in most things, but not in this. You see, even if nothing had happened, he wouldn't like to lose me just yet, because of Norah."

"Norah?"

"My sister. She's going to be married in October. I wonder if we shall ever be as happy as they will."

"Happy! They will be miserable compared with us. Not that I know who the man is."

"Why, Tom of course. Do you mean to say you really didn't know?"

"Tom! Tom Chase?"

"Of course."

I gasped.

"Well, I'm hanged," I said. "When I think of the torments I've been through because of that wretched man, and all for nothing, I don't know what to say."

"Don't you like Tom?"

"Very much. I always did. But I was awfully jealous of him."

"You weren't! How silly of you."

"Of course I was. He was always about with you, and called you Phyllis, and generally behaved as if you and he were the heroine and hero of a musical comedy, so what else could I think? I heard you singing duets after dinner once. I drew the worst conclusions."

"When was that? What were you doing there?"

"It was shortly after Ukridge had got on your father's nerves, and nipped our acquaintance in the bud. I used to come every night to the hedge opposite your drawing-room window, and brood there by the hour."

"Poor old boy!"

"Hoping to hear you sing. And when you did sing, and he joined in all flat, I used to swear. You'll probably find most of the bark scorched off the tree I leaned against."

"Poor old man! Still, it's all over now, isn't it?"

"And when I was doing my very best to show off before you at tennis, you went away just as I got into form."

"I'm very sorry, but I couldn't know, could I? I thought you always played like that."

"I know. I knew you would. It nearly turned my hair white. I didn't see how a girl could ever care for a man who was so bad at tennis."

"One doesn't love a man because he's good at tennis."

"What *does* a girl see to love in a man?" I inquired abruptly; and paused on the verge of a great discovery.

"Oh, I don't know," she replied, most unsatisfactorily.

And I could draw no views from her.

"But about father," said she. "What *are* we to do?"

"He objects to me."

"He's perfectly furious with you."

"Blow, blow," I said, "thou winter wind. Thou are not so unkind—"

"He'll never forgive you."

"—As man's ingratitude. I saved his life. At the risk of my own. Why I believe I've got a legal claim on him. Who ever heard of a man having his life saved, and not being delighted when his preserver wanted to marry his daughter? Your father is striking at the very root of the short-story writer's little earnings. He mustn't be allowed to do it."

"Jerry!"

I started.

"Again!" I said.

"What?"

"Say it again. Do, please. Now."

"Very well. Jerry!"

"It was the first time you had called me by my Christian name. I don't suppose you've the remotest notion how splendid it sounds when you say it. There is something poetical, almost holy, about it."

"Jerry, please!"

"Say on."

"Do be sensible. Don't you see how serious this is? We must think how we can make father consent."

"All right," I said. "We'll tackle the point. I'm sorry to be frivolous, but I'm so happy I can't keep it all in. I've got you and I can't think of anything else."

"Try."

"I'll pull myself together. . . Now, say on once more."

"We can't marry without his consent."

"Why not?" I said, not having a marked respect for the professor's whims. "Gretna Green is out of date, but there are registrars."

"I hate the very idea of a registrar," she said with decision. "Besides—"

"Well?"

"Poor father would never get over it. We've always been such friends. If I married against his wishes, he would—oh, you know. Not let me near him again, and not write to me. And he would hate it all the time he was doing it. He would be bored to death without me."

"Who wouldn't?" I said.

"Because, you see, Norah has never been quite the same. She has spent such a lot of her time on visits to people, that she and father don't understand each other so well as he and I do. She would try and be nice to him, but she wouldn't know him as I do. And, besides, she will be with him such a little, now she's going to be married."

"But, look here," I said, "this is absurd. You say your father would never see you again, and so on, if you married me. Why? It's nonsense. It isn't as if I were a sort of social outcast. We were the best of friends till that man Hawk gave me away like that."

"I know. But he's very obstinate about some things. You see, he thinks the whole thing has made him look ridiculous, and it will take him a long time to forgive you for that."

I realised the truth of this. One can pardon any injury to oneself, unless it hurts one's vanity. Moreover, even in a genuine case of rescue, the rescued man must always feel a little aggrieved with his rescuer, when he thinks the matter over in cold blood. He must regard him unconsciously as the super regards the actor-manager, indebted to him for the means of supporting existence, but grudging him the limelight and the centre of the stage and the applause. Besides, every one instinctively dislikes being under an obligation which they can never wholly repay. And when a man discovers that he has experienced all these mixed sensations for nothing, as the professor had done, his wrath is likely to be no slight thing.

Taking everything into consideration, I could not but feel that it would require more than a little persuasion to make the professor bestow his blessing with that genial warmth which we like to see in our fathers-in-law's elect.

"You don't think," I said, "that time, the Great Healer, and so on—? He won't feel kindlier disposed towards me—say in a month's time?"

"Of course he *might*," said Phyllis; but she spoke doubtfully.

"He strikes me from what I have seen of him as a man of moods. I might do something one of these days which would completely alter his views. We will hope for the best."

"About telling father—?"

"Need we, do you think?" I said.

"Yes, we must. I couldn't bear to think that I was keeping it from him. I don't think I've ever kept anything from him in my life. Nothing bad, I mean."

"You count this among your darker crimes, then?"

"I was looking at it from father's point of view. He will be awfully angry. I don't know how I shall begin telling him."

"Good heavens!" I cried, "you surely don't think I'm going to let you do that! Keep safely out of the way while you tell him! Not much. I'm coming back with you now, and we'll break the bad news together."

"No, not tonight. He may be tired and rather cross. We had better wait till tomorrow. You might speak to him in the morning."

"Where shall I find him?"

"He is certain to go to the beach before breakfast for a swim."

"Good. I'll be there."

"Ukridge," I said, when I got back, "I want your advice."

It stirred him like a trumpet blast. I suppose, when a man is in the habit of giving unsolicited counsel to everyone he meets, it is as invigorating as an electric shock to him to be asked for it spontaneously.

"Bring it out, laddie!" he replied cordially. "I'm with you. Here, come along into the garden, and state your case."

This suited me. It is always easier to talk intimately in the dark, and I did not wish to be interrupted by the sudden entrance of the Hired

Man or Mrs. Beale, of which there was always a danger indoors. We walked down to the paddock. Ukridge lit a cigar.

"Ukridge," I said, "I'm engaged!"

"What!" A huge hand whistled through the darkness and smote me heavily between the shoulder-blades. "By Jove, old boy, I wish you luck. 'Pon my Sam I do! Best thing in the world for you. Bachelors are mere excrescences. Never knew what happiness was till I married. When's the wedding to be?"

"That's where I want your advice. What you might call a difficulty has arisen about the wedding. It's like this. I'm engaged to Phyllis Derrick."

"Derrick? Derrick?"

"You can't have forgotten her! Good Lord, what eyes some men have! Why, if I'd only seen her once, I should have remembered her all my life."

"I know, now. Rather a pretty girl, with blue eyes."

I stared at him blankly. It was not much good, as he could not see my face, but it relieved me. "Rather a pretty girl!" What a description!

"Of course, yes," continued Ukridge. "She came to dinner here one night with her father, that fat little buffer."

"As you were careful to call him to his face at the time, confound you! It was that that started all the trouble."

"Trouble? What trouble?"

"Why, her father. . ."

"By Jove, I remember now! So worried lately, old boy, that my memory's gone groggy. Of course! Her father fell into the sea, and you fished him out. Why, damme, it's like the stories you read."

"It's also very like the stories I used to write. But they had one point about them which this story hasn't. They invariably ended happily, with the father joining the hero's and heroine's hands and giving his blessing. Unfortunately, in the present case, that doesn't seem likely to happen."

"The old man won't give his consent?"

"I'm afraid not. I haven't asked him yet, but the chances are against it."

"But why? What's the matter with you? You're an excellent chap, sound in wind and limb, and didn't you once tell me that, if you married, you came into a pretty sizeable bit of money?"

"Yes, I do. That part of it is all right."

Ukridge's voice betrayed perplexity.

"I don't understand this thing, old horse," he said. "I should have thought the old boy would have been all over you. Why, damme, I never heard of anything like it. You saved his life! You fished him out of the water."

"After chucking him in. That's the trouble."

"You chucked him in?"

"By proxy."

I explained. Ukridge, I regret to say, laughed in a way that must have been heard miles away in distant villages in Devonshire.

"You devil!" he bellowed. "'Pon my Sam, old horse, to look at you one would never have thought you'd have had it in you."

"I can't help looking respectable."

"What are you going to do about it?"

"That's where I wanted your advice. You're a man of resource. What would you do in my place?"

Ukridge tapped me impressively on the shoulder.

"Laddie," he said, "there's one thing that'll carry you through any mess."

"And that is—?"

"Cheek, my boy, cheek. Gall. Nerve. Why, take my case. I never told you how I came to marry, did I. I thought not. Well, it was this way. It'll do you a bit of good, perhaps, to hear the story, for, mark you, blessings weren't going cheap in my case either. You know Millie's Aunt Elizabeth, the female who wrote that letter? Well, when I tell you that she was Millie's nearest relative and that it was her consent I had to snaffle, you'll see that I was faced with a bit of a problem."

"Let's have it," I said.

"Well, the first time I ever saw Millie was in a first-class carriage on the underground. I'd got a third-class ticket, by the way. The carriage was full, and I got up and gave her my seat, and, as I hung suspended over her by a strap, damme, I fell in love with her then and there. You've no conception, laddie, how indescribably ripping she looked, in a sort of blue dress with a bit of red in it and a hat with thingummies. Well, we both got out at South Kensington. By that time I was gasping for air and saw that the thing wanted looking into. I'd never had much time to bother about women, but I realised that this must not be missed. I was in love, old horse. It comes over you quite suddenly, like a tidal wave. . ."

"I know! I know! Good Heavens, you can't tell me anything about that."

"Well, I followed her. She went to a house in Thurloe Square. I waited outside and thought it over. I had got to get into that shanty and make her acquaintance, if they threw me out on my ear. So I rang the bell. 'Is Lady Lichenhall at home?' I asked. You spot the devilish cunning of the ruse, what? My asking for a female with a title was to make 'em think I was one of the Upper Ten."

"How were you dressed?" I could not help asking.

"Oh, it was one of my frock-coat days. I'd been to see a man about tutoring his son, and by a merciful dispensation of Providence there was a fellow living in the same boarding-house with me who was about my build and had a frock-coat, and he had lent it to me. At least, he hadn't exactly lent it to me, but I knew where he kept it and he was out at the time. There was nothing the matter with my appearance. Quite the young duke, I assure you, laddie, down to the last button. 'Is Lady Lichenhall at home?' I asked. 'No,' said the maid, 'nobody of that name here. This is Lady Lakenheath's house.' So, you see, I had a bit of luck at the start, because the names were a bit alike. Well, I got the maid to show me in somehow, and, once in you can bet I talked for all I was worth. Kept up a flow of conversation about being misdirected and coming to the wrong house. Went away, and called a few days later. Gradually wormed my way in. Called regularly. Spied on their movements, met 'em at every theatre they went to, and bowed, and finally got away with Millie before her aunt knew what was happening or who I was or what I was doing or anything."

"And what's the moral?"

"Why, go in like a mighty, rushing wind! Bustle 'em! Don't give 'em a moment's rest or time to think or anything. Why, if I'd given Millie's Aunt Elizabeth time to think, where should we have been? Not at Combe Regis together, I'll bet. You heard that letter, and know what she thinks of me now, on reflection. If I'd gone slow and played a timid waiting-game, she'd have thought that before I married Millie, instead of afterwards. I give you my honest word, laddie, that there was a time, towards the middle of our acquaintance—after she had stopped mixing me up with the man who came to wind the clocks—when that woman ate out of my hand! Twice—on two separate occasions—she actually asked my advice about feeding her toy Pomeranian! Well, that shows you! Bustle 'em, laddie! Bustle 'em!"

"Ukridge," I said, "you inspire me. You would inspire a caterpillar. I will go to the professor—I was going anyhow, but now I shall go aggressively. I will prise a father's blessing out of him, if I have to do it with a crowbar."

"That's the way to talk, old horse. Don't beat about the bush. Tell him exactly what you want and stand no nonsense. If you don't see what you want in the window, ask for it. Where did you think of tackling him?"

"Phyllis tells me that he always goes for a swim before breakfast. I thought of going down tomorrow and waylaying him."

"You couldn't do better. By Jove!" said Ukridge suddenly. "I'll tell you what I'll do, laddie. I wouldn't do it for everybody, but I look on you as a favourite son. I'll come with you, and help break the ice."

"What!"

"Don't you be under any delusion, old horse," said Ukridge paternally. "You haven't got an easy job in front of you and what you'll need more than anything else, when you really get down to brass-tacks, is a wise, kindly man of the world at your elbow, to whoop you on when your nerve fails you and generally stand in your corner and see that you get a fair show."

"But it's rather an intimate business. . ."

"Never mind! Take my tip and have me at your side. I can say things about you that you would be too modest to say for yourself. I can plead your case, laddie. I can point out in detail all that the old boy will be missing if he gives you the miss-in-baulk. Well, that's settled, then. About eight tomorrow morning, what? I'll be there, my boy. A swim will do me good."

XIX

Asking Papa

Reviewing the matter later, I could see that I made one or two blunders in my conduct of the campaign to win over Professor Derrick. In the first place, I made a bad choice of time and place. At the moment this did not strike me. It is a simple matter, I reflected, for a man to pass another by haughtily and without recognition, when they meet on dry land; but, when the said man, being it should be remembered, an indifferent swimmer, is accosted in the water and out of his depth, the feat becomes a hard one. It seemed to me that I should have a better chance with the professor in the water than out of it.

My second mistake—and this was brought home to me almost immediately—was in bringing Ukridge along. Not that I really brought him along; it was rather a case of being unable to shake him off. When he met me on the gravel outside the house at a quarter to eight on the following morning, clad in a dingy mackintosh which, swinging open, revealed a purple bathing-suit, I confess that my heart sank. Unfortunately, all my efforts to dissuade him from accompanying me were attributed by him to a pardonable nervousness—or, as he put it, to the needle.

"Buck up, laddie!" he roared encouragingly. "I had anticipated this. Something seemed to tell me that your nerve would go when it came to the point. You're deuced lucky, old horse, to have a man like me at your side. Why, if you were alone, you wouldn't have a word to say for yourself. You'd just gape at the man and yammer. But I'm with you laddie, I'm with you. If your flow of conversation dries up, count on me to keep the thing going."

And so it came about that, having reached the Cob and spying in the distance the grey head of the professor bobbing about on the face of the waters, we dived in and swam rapidly towards him.

His face was turned in the opposite direction when we came up with him. He was floating peacefully on his back, and it was plain that he had not observed our approach. For when, treading water easily in his rear, I wished him good morning in my most conciliatory tone, he stood not upon the order of his sinking, but went under like so much pig-iron.

I waited courteously until he rose to the surface again, when I repeated my remark.

He expelled the last remnant of water from his mouth with a wrathful splutter, and cleared his eyes with the back of his hand. I confess to a slight feeling of apprehension as I met his gaze. Nor was my uneasiness diminished by the spectacle of Ukridge splashing tactfully in the background like a large seal. Ukridge so far had made no remarks. He had dived in very flat, and I imagine that his breath had not yet returned to him. He had the air of one who intends to get used to his surroundings before trusting himself to speech.

"The water is delightfully warm," I said.

"Oh, it's you!" said the professor; and I could not cheat myself into the belief that he spoke cordially. Ukridge snorted loudly in the offing. The professor turned sharply, as if anxious to observe this marine phenomenon; and the annoyed gurgle which he gave showed that he was not approving of Ukridge either. I did not approve of Ukridge myself. I wished he had not come. Ukridge, in the water, lacks dignity. I felt that he prejudiced my case.

"You are swimming splendidly this morning," I went on perseveringly, feeling that an ounce of flattery is worth a pound of rhetoric. "If," I added, "you will allow me to say so."

"I will not!" he snapped. "I—" here a small wave, noticing that his mouth was open, stepped in. "I wish," he resumed warmly, "as I said in me letter, to have nothing to do with you. I consider that ye've behaved in a manner that can only be described as abominable, and I will thank you to leave me alone."

"But allow me—"

"I will not allow ye, sir. I will allow ye nothing. Is it not enough to make me the laughing-stock, the butt, sir, of this town, without pursuing me in this way when I wish to enjoy a quiet swim?"

"Now, laddie, laddie," said Ukridge, placing a large hand on his shoulder, "these are harsh words! Be reasonable! Think before you speak. You little know. . ."

"Go to the devil!" said the professor. "I wish to have nothing to do with either of you. I should be glad if you would cease this persecution. Persecution, sir!"

His remarks, which I have placed on paper as if they were continuous and uninterrupted, were punctuated in reality by a series of gasps and puffings, as he received and rejected the successors of the wave he had swallowed at the beginning of our little chat. The art of conducting conversation while in the water is not given to every swimmer. This he seemed to realise, for, as if to close the interview, he proceeded to make his way as quickly as he could to the shore. Unfortunately, his first dash brought him squarely up against Ukridge, who, not having expected the collision, clutched wildly at him and took him below the surface again. They came up a moment later on the worst terms.

"Are you trying to drown me, sir?" barked the professor.

"My dear old horse," said Ukridge complainingly, "it's a little hard. You might look where you're going."

"You grappled with me!"

"You took me by surprise, laddie. Rid yourself of the impression that you're playing water-polo."

"But, professor," I said, joining the group and treading water, "one moment."

I was growing annoyed with the man. I could have ducked him, but for the reflection that my prospects of obtaining his consent to my engagement would scarcely have been enhanced thereby.

"But, professor," I said, "one moment."

"Go away, sir! I have nothing to say to you."

"But he has lots to say to you," said Ukridge. "Now's the time, old horse," he added encouragingly to me. "Spill the news!"

Without preamble I gave out the text of my address.

"I love your daughter, Phyllis, Mr. Derrick. She loves me. In fact, we are engaged."

"Devilish well put, laddie," said Ukridge approvingly.

The professor went under as if he had been seized with cramp. It was a little trying having to argue with a man, of whom one could not predict with certainty that at any given moment he would not be under water. It tended to spoil the flow of one's eloquence. The best of arguments is useless if the listener suddenly disappears in the middle of it.

"Stick to it, old horse," said Ukridge. "I think you're going to bring it off."

I stuck to it.

"Mr. Derrick," I said, as his head emerged, "you are naturally surprised."

"You would be," said Ukridge. "We don't blame you," he added handsomely.

"You—you—you—" So far from cooling the professor, liberal doses of water seemed to make him more heated. "You impudent scoundrel!"

My reply was more gentlemanly, more courteous, on a higher plane altogether.

I said, winningly: "Cannot we let bygones be bygones?"

From his remarks I gathered that we could not. I continued. I was under the unfortunate necessity of having to condense my speech. I was not able to let myself go as I could have wished, for time was an important consideration. Ere long, swallowing water at his present rate, the professor must inevitably become waterlogged.

"I have loved your daughter," I said rapidly, "ever since I first saw her. . ."

"And he's a capital chap," interjected Ukridge. "One of the best. Known him for years. You'll like him."

"I learned last night that she loved me. But she will not marry me without your consent. Stretch your arms out straight from the shoulders and fill your lungs well and you can't sink. So I have come this morning to ask for your consent."

"Give it!" advised Ukridge. "Couldn't do better. A very sound fellow. Pots of money, too. At least he will have when he marries."

"I know we have not been on the best of terms lately. For Heaven's sake don't try to talk, or you'll sink. The fault," I said, generously, "was mine. . ."

"Well put," said Ukridge.

"But when you have heard my explanation, I am sure you will forgive me. There, I told you so."

He reappeared some few feet to the left. I swam up, and resumed.

"When you left us so abruptly after our little dinner-party—"

"Come again some night," said Ukridge cordially. "Any time you're passing."

". . . you put me in a very awkward position. I was desperately in love with your daughter, and as long as you were in the frame of mind in which you left I could not hope to find an opportunity of revealing my feelings to her."

"Revealing feelings is good," said Ukridge approvingly. "Neat."

"You see what a fix I was in, don't you? Keep your arms well out. I thought for hours and hours, to try and find some means of bringing about a reconciliation. You wouldn't believe how hard I thought."

"Got as thin as a corkscrew," said Ukridge.

"At last, seeing you fishing one morning when I was on the Cob, it struck me all of a sudden. . ."

"You know how it is," said Ukridge.

". . . all of a sudden that the very best way would be to arrange a little boating accident. I was confident that I could rescue you all right."

Here I paused, and he seized the opportunity to curse me—briefly, with a wary eye on an incoming wavelet.

"If it hadn't been for the inscrutable workings of Providence, which has a mania for upsetting everything, all would have been well. In fact, all was well till you found out."

"Always the way," said Ukridge sadly. "Always the way."

"You young blackguard!"

He managed to slip past me, and made for the shore.

"Look at the thing from the standpoint of a philosopher, old horse," urged Ukridge, splashing after him. "The fact that the rescue was arranged oughtn't to matter. I mean to say, you didn't know it at the time, so, relatively, it was not, and you were genuinely saved from a watery grave and all that sort of thing."

I had not imagined Ukridge capable of such an excursion into metaphysics. I saw the truth of his line of argument so clearly that it seemed to me impossible for anyone else to get confused over it. I had certainly pulled the professor out of the water, and the fact that I had first caused him to be pushed in had nothing to do with the case. Either a man is a gallant rescuer or he is not a gallant rescuer. There is no middle course. I had saved his life—for he would certainly have drowned if left to himself—and I was entitled to his gratitude. That was all there was to be said about it.

These things both Ukridge and I tried to make plain as we swam along. But whether it was that the salt water he had swallowed had dulled the professor's normally keen intelligence or that our power of stating a case was too weak, the fact remains that he reached the beach an unconvinced man.

"Then may I consider," I said, "that your objections are removed? I have your consent?"

He stamped angrily, and his bare foot came down on a small, sharp pebble. With a brief exclamation he seized his foot in one hand and hopped up the beach. While hopping, he delivered his ultimatum. Probably the only instance on record of a father adopting this attitude in dismissing a suitor.

"You may not!" he cried. "You may consider no such thing. My objections were never more absolute. You detain me in the water, sir, till I am blue, sir, blue with cold, in order to listen to the most preposterous and impudent nonsense I ever heard."

This was unjust. If he had listened attentively from the first and avoided interruptions and had not behaved like a submarine we should have got through the business in half the time.

I said so.

"Don't talk to me, sir," he replied, hobbling off to his dressing-tent. "I will not listen to you. I will have nothing to do with you. I consider you impudent, sir."

"I assure you it was unintentional."

"Isch!" he said—being the first occasion and the last on which I have ever heard that remarkable monosyllable proceed from the mouth of a man. And he vanished into his tent.

"Laddie," said Ukridge solemnly, "do you know what I think?"

"Well?"

"You haven't clicked, old horse!" said Ukridge.

XX

Scientific Golf

People are continually writing to the papers—or it may be one solitary enthusiast who writes under a number of pseudonyms—on the subject of sport, and the over-doing of the same by the modern young man. I recall one letter in which "Efficiency" gave it as his opinion that if the Young Man played less golf and did more drill, he would be all the better for it. I propose to report my doings with the professor on the links at some length, in order to refute this absurd view. Everybody ought to play golf, and nobody can begin it too soon. There ought not to be a single able-bodied infant in the British Isles who has not foozled a drive. To take my case. Suppose I had employed in drilling the hours I had spent in learning to handle my clubs. I might have drilled before the professor by the week without softening his heart. I might have ported arms and grounded arms and presented arms, and generally behaved in the manner advocated by "Efficiency," and what would have been the result? Indifference on his part, or—and if I overdid the thing—irritation. Whereas, by devoting a reasonable portion of my youth to learning the intricacies of golf I was enabled. . .

It happened in this way.

To me, as I stood with Ukridge in the fowl-run in the morning following my maritime conversation with the professor, regarding a hen that had posed before us, obviously with a view to inspection, there appeared a man carrying an envelope. Ukridge, who by this time saw, as Calverley almost said, "under every hat a dun," and imagined that no envelope could contain anything but a small account, softly and silently vanished away, leaving me to interview the enemy.

"Mr. Garnet, sir?" said the foe.

I recognised him. He was Professor Derrick's gardener.

I opened the envelope. No. Father's blessings were absent. The letter was in the third person. Professor Derrick begged to inform Mr. Garnet that, by defeating Mr. Saul Potter, he had qualified for the final round of the Combe Regis Golf Tournament, in which, he understood, Mr. Garnet was to be his opponent. If it would be convenient for Mr. Garnet to play off the match on the present afternoon, Professor Derrick would be obliged if he would be at the Club House at half-past two. If this hour and day were unsuitable, would he kindly arrange others. The bearer would wait.

The bearer did wait. He waited for half-an-hour, as I found it impossible to shift him, not caring to use violence on a man well stricken in years, without first plying him with drink. He absorbed more of our diminishing cask of beer than we could conveniently spare, and then trudged off with a note, beautifully written in the third person, in which Mr. Garnet, after numerous compliments and thanks, begged to inform Professor Derrick that he would be at the Club House at the hour mentioned.

"And," I added—to myself, not in the note—"I will give him such a licking that he'll brain himself with a cleek."

For I was not pleased with the professor. I was conscious of a malicious joy at the prospect of snatching the prize from him. I knew he had set his heart on winning the tournament this year. To be runner-up two years in succession stimulates the desire for first place. It would be doubly bitter to him to be beaten by a newcomer, after the absence of his rival, the colonel, had awakened hope in him. And I knew I could do it. Even allowing for bad luck—and I am never a very unlucky golfer—I could rely almost with certainty on crushing the man.

"And I'll do it," I said to Bob, who had trotted up. I often make Bob the recipient of my confidences. He listens appreciatively, and never interrupts. And he never has grievances of his own. If there is one person I dislike, it is the man who tries to air his grievances when I wish to air mine.

"Bob," I said, running his tail through my fingers, "listen to me, my old University chum, for I have matured a dark scheme. Don't run away. You know you don't really want to go and look at that chicken. Listen to me. If I am in form this afternoon, and I feel in my bones that I shall be, I shall nurse the professor. I shall play with him. Do you understand the principles of Match play at Golf, Robert? You score by holes, not strokes. There are eighteen holes. All right, how was *I* to know that you knew that without my telling you? Well, if you understand so much about the game, you will appreciate my dark scheme. I shall toy with the professor, Bob. I shall let him get ahead, and then catch him up. I shall go ahead myself, and let him catch me up. I shall race him neck and neck till the very end. Then, when his hair has turned white with the strain, and he's lost a couple of stone in weight, and his eyes are starting out of his head, and he's praying—if he ever does pray—to the Gods of Golf that he may be allowed to win, I shall go ahead and beat him by a hole. *I'll* teach him, Robert. He shall taste of my despair, and learn by proof in some wild hour how much the wretched dare. And when it's all over, and he's torn all his hair out and smashed all his clubs, I shall go and commit suicide off the Cob. Because, you see, if I can't marry Phyllis, I shan't have any use for life."

Bob wagged his tail cheerfully.

"I mean it," I said, rolling him on his back and punching him on the chest till his breathing became stertorous. "You don't see the sense of it, I know. But then you've got none of the finer feelings. You're a jolly good dog, Robert, but you're a rank materialist. Bones and cheese and potatoes with gravy over them make you happy. You don't know what it is to be in love. You'd better get right side up now, or you'll have apoplexy."

It has been my aim in the course of this narrative to extenuate nothing, nor set down aught in malice. Like the gentleman who played euchre with the Heathen Chinee, I state but facts. I do not, therefore, slur over my scheme for disturbing the professor's peace of mind. I am not always good and noble. I am the hero of this story, but I have my off moments.

I felt ruthless towards the professor. I cannot plead ignorance of the golfer's point of view as an excuse for my plottings. I knew that to one whose soul is in the game as the professor's was, the agony of being just beaten in an important match exceeds in bitterness all other agonies. I knew that, if I scraped through by the smallest possible margin, his appetite would be destroyed, his sleep o' nights broken. He would wake from fitful slumber moaning that if he had only used his iron instead of his mashie at the tenth, all would have been well; that, if he had putted more carefully on the seventh green, life would not be drear and blank; that a more judicious manipulation of his brassey throughout might have given him something to live for. All these things I knew.

And they did not touch me. I was adamant. The professor was waiting for me at the Club House, and greeted me with a cold and stately inclination of the head.

"Beautiful day for golf," I observed in my gay, chatty manner. He bowed in silence.

"Very well," I thought. "Wait. Just wait."

"Miss Derrick is well, I hope?" I added, aloud.

That drew him. He started. His aspect became doubly forbidding.

"Miss Derrick is perfectly well, sir, I thank you."

"And you? No bad effect, I hope, from your dip yesterday?"

"Mr. Garnet, I came here for golf, not conversation," he said.

We made it so. I drove off from the first tee. It was a splendid drive. I should not say so if there were any one else to say so for me. Modesty would forbid. But, as there is no one, I must repeat the statement. It was one of the best drives of my experience. The ball flashed through the air, took the bunker with a dozen feet to spare, and rolled on to the green. I had felt all along that I should be in form. Unless my opponent was equally above himself, he was a lost man. I could toy with him.

The excellence of my drive had not been without its effect on the professor. I could see that he was not confident. He addressed his ball more strangely and at greater length than any one I had ever seen. He waggled his club over it as if he were going to perform a conjuring trick. Then he struck, and topped it.

The ball rolled two yards.

He looked at it in silence. Then he looked at me—also in silence.

I was gazing seawards.

When I looked round he was getting to work with a brassey.

This time he hit the bunker, and rolled back. He repeated this manoeuvre twice.

"Hard luck!" I murmured sympathetically on the third occasion, thereby going as near to being slain with a niblick as it has ever been my lot to go. Your true golfer is easily roused in times of misfortune; and there was a red gleam in the eye of the professor turned to me.

"I shall pick my ball up," he growled.

We walked on in silence to the second tee. He did the second hole in four, which was good. I did it in three, which—unfortunately for him—was better.

I won the third hole.

I won the fourth hole.

I won the fifth hole.

I glanced at my opponent out of the corner of my eyes. The man was suffering. Beads of perspiration stood out on his forehead.

His play had become wilder and wilder at each hole in arithmetical progression. If he had been a plough he could hardly have turned up more soil. The imagination recoiled from the thought of what he could be doing in another half-hour if he deteriorated at his present speed.

A feeling of calm and content stole over me. I was not sorry for him. All the viciousness of my nature was uppermost in me. Once, when he missed the ball clean at the fifth tee, his eye met mine, and we stood staring at each other for a full half-minute without moving. I believe, if I had smiled then, he would have attacked me without hesitation. There is a type of golfer who really almost ceases to be human under stress of the wild agony of a series of foozles.

The sixth hole involves the player in a somewhat tricky piece of cross-country work, owing to the fact that there is a nasty ditch to be negotiated some fifty yards from the green. It is a beast of a ditch, which, if you are out of luck, just catches your second shot. "All hope abandon ye who enter here" might be written on a notice board over it.

The professor entered there. The unhappy man sent his second, as nice and clean a brassey shot as he had made all day, into its very jaws. And then madness seized him. A merciful local rule, framed by kindly men who have been in that ditch themselves, enacts that in such a case the player may take his ball and throw it over his shoulder, losing a stroke. But once, so the legend runs, a scratch man who found himself trapped, scorning to avail himself of this rule at the expense of its accompanying penalty, wrought so shrewdly with his niblick that he not only got out but actually laid his ball dead: and now optimists sometimes imitate his gallantry, though no one yet has been able to imitate his success.

The professor decided to take a chance: and he failed miserably. As I was on the green with my third, and, unless I putted extremely poorly, was morally certain to be down in five, which is bogey for the hole, there was not much practical use in his continuing to struggle. But he did in a spirit of pure vindictiveness, as if he were trying to take it out of the ball. It was a grisly sight to see him, head and shoulders above the ditch, hewing at his obstinate colonel. It was a similar spectacle that once induced a lay spectator of a golf match to observe that he considered hockey a silly game.

"*Sixteen!*" said the professor between his teeth. Then he picked up his ball.

I won the seventh hole.

I won the eighth hole.

The ninth we halved, for in the black depths of my soul I had formed a plan of fiendish subtlety. I intended to allow him to win—with extreme labour—eight holes in succession.

Then, when hope was once more strong in him, I would win the last, and he would go mad.

I watched him carefully as we trudged on. Emotions chased one another across his face. When he won the tenth hole he merely refrained from oaths. When he won the eleventh a sort of sullen pleasure showed in his face. It was at the thirteenth that I detected the first dawning of hope. From then onward it grew.

When, with a sequence of shocking shots, he took the seventeenth hole in seven, he was in a parlous condition. His run of success had engendered within him a desire for conversation. He wanted, as it were, to flap his wings and crow. I could see Dignity wrestling with Talkativeness. I gave him the lead.

"You have got your form now," I said.

Talkativeness had it. Dignity retired hurt. Speech came from him in a rush. When he brought off an excellent drive from the eighteenth tee, he seemed to forget everything.

"Me dear boy,"—he began; and stopped abruptly in some confusion. Silence once more brooded over us as we played ourselves up the fairway and on to the green.

He was on the green in four. I reached it in three. His sixth stroke took him out.

I putted carefully to the very mouth of the hole.

I walked up to my ball and paused. I looked at the professor. He looked at me.

"Go on," he said hoarsely.

Suddenly a wave of compassion flooded over me. What right had I to torture the man like this?

"Professor," I said.

"Go on," he repeated.

"That looks a simple shot," I said, eyeing him steadily, "but I might miss it."

He started.

"And then you would win the Championship."

He dabbed at his forehead with a wet ball of a handkerchief.

"It would be very pleasant for you after getting so near it the last two years."

"Go on," he said for the third time. But there was a note of hesitation in his voice.

"Sudden joy," I said, "would almost certainly make me miss it."

We looked at each other. He had the golf fever in his eyes.

"If," I said slowly, lifting my putter, "you were to give your consent to my marriage with Phyllis—"

He looked from me to the ball, from the ball to me, and back to the ball. It was very, very near the hole.

"Why not?" I said.

He looked up, and burst into a roar of laughter.

"You young devil," said he, smiting his thigh, "you young devil, you've beaten me."

"On the contrary," I said, "you have beaten me."

I LEFT THE PROFESSOR AT the Club House and raced back to the farm. I wanted to pour my joys into a sympathetic ear. Ukridge, I knew, would offer that same sympathetic ear. A good fellow, Ukridge. Always interested in what you had to tell him; never bored.

"Ukridge!" I shouted.

No answer.

I flung open the dining-room door. Nobody.

I went into the drawing-room. It was empty. I drew the garden, and his bedroom. He was not in either.

"He must have gone for a stroll," I said.

I rang the bell.

The Hired Retainer appeared, calm and imperturbable as ever.

"Sir?"

"Oh, where is Mr. Ukridge, Beale?"

"Mr. Ukridge, sir," said the Hired Retainer nonchalantly, "has gone."

"Gone!"

"Yes, sir. Mr. Ukridge and Mrs. Ukridge went away together by the three o'clock train."

XXI

The Calm Before the Storm

B eale," I said, "are you drunk?"

"Wish I was, sir," said the Hired Man.

"Then what on earth do you mean? Gone? Where have they gone to?"

"Don't know, sir. London, I expect."

"London? Why?"

"Don't know, sir."

"When did they go? Oh, you told me that. Didn't they say why they were going?"

"No, sir."

"Didn't you ask! When you saw them packing up and going to the station, didn't you do anything?"

"No, sir."

"Why on earth not?"

"I didn't see them, sir. I only found out as they'd gone after they'd been and went, sir. Walking down by the Net and Mackerel, met one of them coastguards. 'Oh,' says he, 'so you're moving?' 'Who's a-moving?' I says to him. 'Well,' he says to me, 'I seen your Mr. Ukridge and his missus get into the three o'clock train for Axminster. I thought as you was all a-moving.' 'Ho,' I says, 'Ho,' wondering, and I goes on. When I gets back, I asks the missus did she see them packing their boxes, and she says, No, she says, they didn't pack no boxes as she knowed of. And blowed if they had, Mr. Garnet, sir."

"What! They didn't pack!"

"No, sir."

We looked at one another.

"Beale," I said.

"Sir?"

"Do you know what I think?"

"Yes, sir."

"They've bolted."

"So I says to the missus, sir. It struck me right off, in a manner of speaking."

"This is awful," I said.

"Yes, sir."

His face betrayed no emotion, but he was one of those men whose expression never varies. It's a way they have in the Army.

"This wants thinking out, Beale," I said.

"Yes, sir."

"You'd better ask Mrs. Beale to give me some dinner, and then I'll think it over."

"Yes, sir."

I was in an unpleasant position. Ukridge by his defection had left me in charge of the farm. I could dissolve the concern, I supposed, if I wished, and return to London, but I particularly desired to remain in Combe Regis. To complete the victory I had won on the links, it was necessary for me to continue as I had begun. I was in the position of a general who has conquered a hostile country, and is obliged to soothe the feelings of the conquered people before his labours can be considered at an end. I had rushed the professor. It must now be my aim to keep him from regretting that he had been rushed. I must, therefore, stick to my post with the tenacity of an able-bodied leech. There would be trouble. Of that I was certain. As soon as the news got about that Ukridge had gone, the deluge would begin. His creditors would abandon their passive tactics, and take active steps. There was a chance that aggressive measures would be confined to the enemy at our gates, the tradesmen of Combe Regis. But the probability was that the news would spread, and the injured merchants of Dorchester and Axminster rush to the scene of hostilities.

I summoned Beale after dinner and held a council of war. It was no time for airy persiflage. I said, "Beale, we're in the cart."

"Sir?"

"Mr. Ukridge going away like this has left me in a most unpleasant position. I would like to talk it over with you. I daresay you know that we—that Mr. Ukridge owes a considerable amount of money round about here to tradesmen?"

"Yes, sir."

"Well, when they find out that he has—er—"

"Shot the moon, sir," suggested the Hired Retainer helpfully.

"Gone up to town," I amended. "When they find out that he has gone up to town, they are likely to come bothering us a good deal."

"Yes, sir."

"I fancy that we shall have them all round here tomorrow. News of this sort always spreads quickly. The point is, then, what are we to do?"

He propounded no scheme, but stood in an easy attitude of attention, waiting for me to continue.

I continued.

"Let's see exactly how we stand," I said. "My point is that I particularly wish to go on living down here for at least another fortnight. Of course, my position is simple. I am Mr. Ukridge's guest. I shall go on living as I have been doing up to the present. He asked me down here to help him look after the fowls, so I shall go on looking after them. Complications set in when we come to consider you and Mrs. Beale. I suppose you won't care to stop on after this?"

The Hired Retainer scratched his chin and glanced out of the window. The moon was up, and the garden looked cool and mysterious in the dim light.

"It's a pretty place, Mr. Garnet, sir," he said.

"It is," I said, "but about other considerations? There's the matter of wages. Are yours in arrears?"

"Yes, sir. A month."

"And Mrs. Beale's the same, I suppose?"

"Yes, sir. A month."

"H'm. Well, it seems to me, Beale, you can't lose anything by stopping on."

"I can't be paid any less than I have bin, sir," he agreed.

"Exactly. And, as you say, it's a pretty place. You might just as well stop on, and help me in the fowl-run. What do you think?"

"Very well, sir."

"And Mrs. Beale will do the same?"

"Yes, sir."

"That's excellent. You're a hero, Beale. I shan't forget you. There's a cheque coming to me from a magazine in another week for a short story. When it arrives, I'll look into that matter of back wages. Tell Mrs. Beale I'm much obliged to her, will you?"

"Yes, sir."

Having concluded that delicate business, I lit my pipe, and strolled out into the garden with Bob. I cursed Ukridge as I walked. It was abominable of him to desert me in this way. Even if I had not been his friend, it would have been bad. The fact that we had known each other for years made it doubly discreditable. He might at least have warned me, and given me the option of leaving the sinking ship with him.

But, I reflected, I ought not to be surprised. His whole career, as long as I had known him, had been dotted with little eccentricities of a type which an unfeeling world generally stigmatises as shady. They were small things, it was true; but they ought to have warned me. We are most of us wise after the event. When the wind has blown, we can generally discover a multitude of straws which should have shown us which way it was blowing.

Once, I remembered, in our schoolmaster days, when guineas, though regular, were few, he had had occasion to increase his wardrobe. If I recollect rightly, he thought he had a chance of a good position in the tutoring line, and only needed good clothes to make it his. He took four pounds of his salary in advance,—he was in the habit of doing this: he never had any salary left by the end of term, it having vanished in advance loans beforehand. With this he was to buy two suits, a hat, new boots, and collars. When it came to making the purchases, he found, what he had overlooked previously in his optimistic way, that four pounds did not go very far. At the time, I remember, I thought his method of grappling with the situation humorous. He bought a hat for three-and-sixpence, and got the suits and the boots on the instalment system, paying a small sum in advance, as earnest of more to come. He then pawned one suit to pay for the first few instalments, and finally departed, to be known no more. His address he had given—with a false name—at an empty house, and when the tailor arrived with his minions of the law, all he found was an annoyed caretaker, and a pile of letters written by himself, containing his bill in its various stages of evolution.

Or again. There was a bicycle and photograph shop near the school. He went into this one day, and his roving eye fell on a tandem bicycle. He did not want a tandem bicycle, but that influenced him not at all. He ordered it provisionally. He also ordered an enlarging camera, a kodak, and a magic lantern. The order was booked, and the goods were to be delivered when he had made up his mind concerning them. After a week the shopman sent round to ask if there were any further particulars which Mr. Ukridge would like to learn before definitely ordering them. Mr. Ukridge sent back word that he was considering the matter, and that in the meantime would he be so good as to let him have that little clockwork man in his window, which walked when wound up? Having got this, and not paid for it, Ukridge thought that he had done handsomely by the bicycle and photograph man, and that things were square between them. The latter met him a few days afterwards, and expostulated plaintively. Ukridge explained. "My good man," he said, "you know, I really think we need say no more about the matter. Really, you're come out of it very well. Now, look here, which would you rather be owed for? A clockwork man—which is broken, and you can have it back—or a tandem bicycle, an enlarging camera, a kodak, and a magic-lantern? What?" His reasoning was too subtle for the uneducated mind. The man retired, puzzled, and unpaid, and Ukridge kept the clockwork toy.

XXII

The Storm Breaks

Rather to my surprise, the next morning passed off uneventfully. Our knocker advertised no dun. Our lawn remained untrodden by hob-nailed boots. By lunch-time I had come to the conclusion that the expected Trouble would not occur that day, and I felt that I might well leave my post for the afternoon, while I went to the professor's to pay my respects. The professor was out when I arrived. Phyllis was in, and it was not till the evening that I started for the farm again.

As I approached, the sound of voices smote my ears.

I stopped. I could hear Beale speaking. Then came the rich notes of Vickers, the butcher. Then Beale again. Then Dawlish the grocer. Then a chorus.

The storm had burst, and in my absence.

I blushed for myself. I was in command, and I had deserted the fort in time of need. What must the faithful Hired Man be thinking of me? Probably he placed me, as he had placed Ukridge, in the ragged ranks of those who have Shot the Moon.

Fortunately, having just come from the professor's I was in the costume which of all my wardrobe was most calculated to impress. To a casual observer I should probably suggest wealth and respectability. I stopped for a moment to cool myself, for, as is my habit when pleased with life, I had been walking fast; then opened the gate and strode in, trying to look as opulent as possible.

It was an animated scene that met my eyes. In the middle of the lawn stood the devoted Beale, a little more flushed than I had seen him hitherto, parleying with a burly and excited young man without a coat. Grouped round the pair were some dozen men, young, middle-aged, and old, all talking their hardest. I could distinguish nothing of what they were saying. I noticed that Beale's left cheekbone was a little discoloured, and there was a hard, dogged expression on his face. He, too, was in his shirt-sleeves.

My entry created no sensation. Nobody, apparently, had heard the latch click, and nobody had caught sight of me. Their eyes were fixed on the young man and Beale. I stood at the gate, and watched them.

There seemed to have been trouble already. Looking more closely, I perceived sitting on the grass apart a second young man. His face was obscured by a dirty pocket handkerchief, with which he dabbed tenderly at his features. Every now and then the shirt-sleeved young man flung his hand towards him with an indignant gesture, talking hard the while. It did not need a preternaturally keen observer to deduce what had happened. Beale must have fallen out with the young man who was sitting on the grass and smitten him; and now his friend had taken up the quarrel.

"Now this," I said to myself, "is rather interesting. Here, in this one farm, we have the only three known methods of dealing with duns. Beale is evidently an exponent of the violent method. Ukridge is an apostle of Evasion. I shall try Conciliation. I wonder which of us will be the most successful."

Meanwhile, not to spoil Beale's efforts by allowing him too little scope for experiment, I refrained from making my presence known, and continued to stand by the gate, an interested spectator.

Things were evidently moving now. The young man's gestures became more vigorous. The dogged look on Beale's face deepened. The comments of the Ring increased in point and pungency.

"What did you hit him for, then?"

The question was put, always the same words and with the same air of quiet triumph, at intervals of thirty seconds by a little man in a snuff-coloured suit with a purple tie. Nobody ever answered him, or appeared to listen to him, but he seemed each time to think that he had clinched the matter and cornered his opponent.

Other voices chimed in.

"You hit him, Charlie. Go on. You hit him."

"We'll have the law."

"Go on, Charlie."

Flushed with the favour of the many-headed, Charlie now proceeded from threats to action. His right fist swung round suddenly. But Beale was on the alert. He ducked sharply, and the next moment Charlie was sitting on the ground beside his fallen friend. A hush fell on the Ring, and the little man in the purple tie was left repeating his formula without support.

I advanced. It seemed to me that the time had come to be conciliatory. Charlie was struggling to his feet, obviously anxious for a second round, and Beale was getting into position once more. In another five minutes conciliation would be out of the question.

"What's all this?" I said.

I may mention here that I do not propose to inflict dialect upon the reader. If he had borne with my narrative thus far, I look on him as a friend, and feel that he deserves consideration. I may not have brought out the fact with sufficient emphasis in the foregoing pages, but nevertheless I protest that I have a conscience. Not so much as a "thiccy" shall he find.

My advent caused a stir. Excited men left Beale, and rallied round me. Charlie, rising to his feet, found himself dethroned from his position of Man of the Moment, and stood blinking at the setting sun and opening and shutting his mouth. There was a buzz of conversation.

"Don't all speak at once, please," I said. "I can't possibly follow what you say. Perhaps you will tell me what you want?"

I singled out a short, stout man in grey. He wore the largest whiskers ever seen on human face.

"It's like this, sir. We all of us want to know where we are."

"I can tell you that," I said, "you're on our lawn, and I should be much obliged if you would stop digging your heels into it."

This was not, I suppose, Conciliation in the strictest and best sense of the word; but the thing had to be said. It is the duty of every good citizen to do his best to score off men with whiskers.

"You don't understand me, sir," he said excitedly. "When I said we didn't know where we were, it was a manner of speaking. We want to know how we stand."

"On your heels," I replied gently, "as I pointed out before."

"I am Brass, sir, of Axminster. My account with Mr. Ukridge is ten pounds eight shillings and fourpence. I want to know—"

The whole strength of the company now joined in.

"You know me, Mr. Garnet. Appleby, in the High—" (Voice lost in the general roar).

". . . and eightpence."

"My account with Mr. Uk. . ."

". . . settle. . ."

"I represent Bodger. . ."

A diversion occurred at this point. Charlie, who had long been eyeing Beale sourly, dashed at him with swinging fists, and was knocked down again. The whole trend of the meeting altered once more, Conciliation became a drug. Violence was what the public wanted. Beale had three fights in rapid succession. I was helpless. Instinct prompted me to join the fray; but prudence told me that such a course would be fatal.

At last, in a lull, I managed to catch the Hired Retainer by the arm, as he drew back from the prostrate form of his latest victim. "Drop it, Beale," I whispered hotly, "drop it. We shall never manage these people if you knock them about. Go indoors, and stay there while I talk to them."

"Mr. Garnet, sir," said he, the light of battle dying out of his eyes, "it's 'ard. It's cruel 'ard. I ain't 'ad a turn-up, not to *call* a turn-up, since I've been a time-expired man. I ain't hitting of 'em, Mr. Garnet, sir, not hard I ain't. That there first one of 'em he played me dirty, hittin' at me when I wasn't looking. They can't say as I started it."

"That's all right, Beale," I said soothingly. "I know it wasn't your fault, and I know it's hard on you to have to stop, but I wish you would go indoors. I must talk to these men, and we shan't have a moment's peace while you're here. Cut along."

"Very well, sir. But it's 'ard. Mayn't I 'ave just one go at that Charlie, Mr. Garnet?" he asked wistfully.

"No, no. Go in."

"And if they goes for you, sir, and tries to wipe the face off you?"

"They won't, they won't. If they do, I'll shout for you."

He went reluctantly into the house, and I turned again to my audience.

"If you will kindly be quiet for a moment—" I said.

"I am Appleby, Mr. Garnet, in the High Street. Mr. Ukridge—"

"Eighteen pounds fourteen shillings—"

"Kindly glance—"

I waved my hands wildly above my head.

"Stop! stop! stop!" I shouted.

The babble continued, but diminished gradually in volume. Through the trees, as I waited, I caught a glimpse of the sea. I wished I was out on the Cob, where beyond these voices there was peace. My head was beginning to ache, and I felt faint for want of food.

"Gentlemen," I cried, as the noise died away.

The latch of the gate clicked. I looked up, and saw a tall thin young man in a frock coat and silk hat enter the garden. It was the first time I had seen the costume in the country.

He approached me.

"Mr. Ukridge, sir?" he said.

"My name is Garnet. Mr. Ukridge is away at the moment."

"I come from Whiteley's, Mr. Garnet. Our Mr. Blenkinsop having written on several occasions to Mr. Ukridge calling his attention to the fact that his account has been allowed to mount to a considerable figure, and having received no satisfactory reply, desired me to visit him. I am sorry that he is not at home."

"So am I," I said with feeling.

"Do you expect him to return shortly?"

"No," I said, "I do not."

He was looking curiously at the expectant band of duns. I forestalled his question.

"Those are some of Mr. Ukridge's creditors," I said. "I am just about to address them. Perhaps you will take a seat. The grass is quite dry. My remarks will embrace you as well as them."

Comprehension came into his eyes, and the natural man in him peeped through the polish.

"Great Scott, has he done a bunk?" he cried.

"To the best of my knowledge, yes," I said.

He whistled.

I turned again to the local talent.

"Gentlemen," I shouted.

"Hear, hear," said some idiot.

"Gentlemen, I intend to be quite frank with you. We must decide just how matters stand between us. (A voice: Where's Ukridge?) Mr. Ukridge left for London suddenly (bitter laughter) yesterday afternoon. Personally I think he will come back very shortly."

Hoots of derision greeted this prophecy. I resumed.

"I fail to see your object in coming here. I have nothing for you. I couldn't pay your bills if I wanted to."

It began to be borne upon me that I was becoming unpopular.

"I am here simply as Mr. Ukridge's guest," I proceeded. After all, why should I spare the man? "I have nothing whatever to do with his business affairs. I refuse absolutely to be regarded as in any way indebted to you. I am sorry for you. You have my sympathy. That is all I can give you, sympathy—and good advice."

Dissatisfaction. I was getting myself disliked. And I had meant to be so conciliatory, to speak to these unfortunates words of cheer which should be as olive oil poured into a wound. For I really did sympathise with them. I considered that Ukridge had used them disgracefully. But I was irritated. My head ached abominably.

"Then am I to tell our Mr. Blenkinsop," asked the frock-coated one, "that the money is not and will not be forthcoming?"

"When next you smoke a quiet cigar with your Mr. Blenkinsop," I replied courteously, "and find conversation flagging, I rather think I *should* say something of the sort."

"We shall, of course, instruct our solicitors at once to institute legal proceedings against your Mr. Ukridge."

"Don't call him my Mr. Ukridge. You can do whatever you please."

"That is your last word on the subject?"

"I hope so. But I fear not."

"Where's our money?" demanded a discontented voice from the crowd.

An idea struck me.

"Beale!" I shouted.

Out came the Hired Retainer at the double. I fancy he thought that his help was needed to save me from my friends.

He slowed down, seeing me as yet unassaulted.

"Sir?" he said.

"Isn't there a case of that whisky left somewhere, Beale?"

I had struck the right note. There was a hush of pleased anticipation among the audience.

"Yes, sir. One."

"Then bring it out here and open it."

Beale looked pained.

"For *them*, sir!" he exclaimed.

"Yes. Hurry up."

He hesitated, then without a word went into the house. A hearty cheer went up as he reappeared with the case. I proceeded indoors in search of glasses and water.

Coming out, I realised my folly in having left Beale alone with our visitors even for a minute. A brisk battle was raging between him and a man whom I did not remember to have seen before. The frock-coated young man was looking on with pale fear stamped upon his face; but the rest of the crowd were shouting advice and encouragement was being given to Beale. How I wondered, had he pacified the mob?

I soon discovered. As I ran up as quickly as I could, hampered as I was by the jugs and glasses, Beale knocked his man out with the clean precision of the experienced boxer; and the crowd explained in chorus that it was the pot-boy, from the Net and Mackerel. Like everything else, the whisky had not been paid for and the pot-boy, arriving just as the case was being opened, had made a gallant effort to save it from being distributed free to his fellow-citizens. By the time he came to, the glasses were circulating merrily; and, on observing this, he accepted the situation philosophically enough, and took his turn and turn about with the others.

Everybody was now in excellent fettle. The only malcontents were Beale, whose heart plainly bled at the waste of good Scotch whisky, and the frock-coated young man, who was still pallid.

I was just congratulating myself, as I eyed the revellers, on having achieved a masterstroke of strategy, when that demon Charlie, his defeat, I suppose, still rankling, made a suggestion. From his point of view a timely and ingenious suggestion.

"We can't see the colour of our money," he said pithily, "but we can have our own back."

That settled it. The battle was over. The most skilful general must sometime recognise defeat. I recognised it then, and threw up my hand. I could do nothing further with them. I had done my best for the farm. I could do no more.

I lit my pipe, and strolled into the paddock.

Chaos followed. Indoors and out-of-doors they raged without check. Even Beale gave the thing up. He knocked Charlie into a flower-bed, and then disappeared in the direction of the kitchen.

It was growing dusk. From inside the house came faint sounds of bibulous mirth, as the sacking party emptied the rooms of their contents. In the fowl-run a hen was crooning sleepily in its coop. It was a very soft, liquid, soothing sound.

Presently out came the invaders with their loot, one with a picture, another with a vase, another bearing the gramophone upside down. They were singing in many keys and times.

Then I heard somebody—Charlie again, it seemed to me—propose a raid on the fowl-run.

The fowls had had their moments of unrest since they had been our property, but what they had gone through with us was peace compared with what befell them then. Not even on the second evening of our visit, when we had run unmeasured miles in pursuit of them, had there been such confusion. Roused abruptly from their beauty-sleep they fled in all directions. Their pursuers, roaring with laughter, staggered after them. They tumbled over one another. The summer evening was made hideous with the noise of them.

"Disgraceful, sir. Is it not disgraceful!" said a voice in my ear.

The young man from Whiteley's stood beside me. He did not look happy. His forehead was damp. Somebody seemed to have stepped on his hat, and his coat was smeared with mould.

I was turning to answer him when from the dusk in the direction of the house came a sudden roar. A passionate appeal to the world in general to tell the speaker what all this meant.

There was only one man of my acquaintance with a voice like that.

I walked without hurry towards him.

"Good evening, Ukridge," I said.

XXIII

After the Storm

A yell of welcome drowned the tumult of the looters.

"Is that you, Garny, old horse? What's up? What's the matter? Has everyone gone mad? Who are those infernal scoundrels in the fowl-run? What are they doing? What's been happening?"

"I have been entertaining a little meeting of your creditors," I said. "And now they are entertaining themselves."

"But what did you let them do it for?"

"What is one amongst so many?"

"Well, 'pon my Sam," moaned Ukridge, as, her sardonic calm laid aside, that sinister hen which we called Aunt Elizabeth flashed past us pursued by the whiskered criminal, "it's a little hard! I can't go away for a day—"

"You certainly can't! You're right there. You can't go away without a word—"

"Without a word? What do you mean? Garny, old boy, pull yourself together. You're over-excited. Do you mean to tell me you didn't get my note?"

"What note?"

"The one I left on the dining-room table."

"There was no note there."

"What!"

I was reminded of the scene that had taken place on the first day of our visit.

"Feel in your pockets," I said.

"Why, damme, here it is!" he said in amazement.

"Of course. Where did you expect it would be? Was it important?"

"Why, it explained the whole thing."

"Then," I said, "I wish you would let me read it. A note like that ought to be worth reading."

"It was telling you to sit tight and not worry about us going away—"

"That's good about worrying. You're a thoughtful chap, Ukridge."

"—because we should be back immediately."

"And what sent you up to town?"

"Why, we went to touch Millie's Aunt Elizabeth."

"Oh!" I said, a light shining on the darkness of my understanding.

"You remember Aunt Elizabeth? The old girl who wrote that letter."

"I know. She called you a gaby."

"And a guffin."

"Yes. I remember thinking her a shrewd and discriminating old lady, with a great gift for character delineation. So you went to touch her?"

"That's it. We had to have more money. So I naturally thought of her. Aunt Elizabeth isn't what you might call an admirer of mine—"

"Bless her for that."

"—but she's very fond of Millie, and would do anything if she's allowed to chuck about a few home-truths before doing it. So we went off together, looked her up at her house, stated our case, and collected the stuff. Millie and I shared the work. She did the asking, while I inquired after the rheumatism. She mentioned the figure that would clear us; I patted the dog. Little beast! Got after me when I wasn't looking and chewed my ankle!"

"Thank Heaven!"

"In the end Millie got the money, and I got the home-truths."

"Did she call you a gaby?"

"Twice. And a guffin three times."

"Your Aunt Elizabeth is beginning to fascinate me. She seems just the sort of woman I would like. Well, you got the money?"

"Rather! And I'll tell you another thing, old horse. I scored heavily at the end of the visit. She'd got to the quoting-proverbs stage by that time. 'Ah, my dear,' she said to Millie. 'Marry in haste, repent at leisure.' Millie stood up to her like a little brick. 'I'm afraid that proverb doesn't apply to me, Aunt Elizabeth,' she said, 'because I haven't repented!' What do you think of that, Laddie?"

"Of course, she *hasn't* had much leisure lately," I agreed.

Ukridge's jaw dropped slightly. But he rallied swiftly.

"Idiot! That wasn't what she meant. Millie's an angel!"

"Of course she is," I said cordially. "She's a precious sight too good for you, you old rotter. You bear that fact steadily in mind, and we'll make something of you yet."

At this point Mrs. Ukridge joined us. She had been exploring the house, and noting the damage done. Her eyes were open to their fullest extent.

"Oh, Mr. Garnet, *couldn't* you have stopped them?"

I felt a worm. Had I done as much as I might have done to stem the tide?

"I'm awfully sorry, Mrs. Ukridge," I said humbly. "I really don't think I could have done much more. We tried every method. Beale had seven fights, and I made a speech on the lawn, but it was all no good. Directly they had finished the whisky—"

Ukridge's cry was like that of a lost spirit.

"They didn't get hold of the whisky!"

"They did! It seemed to me that it would smooth things down a little if I served it out. The mob had begun to get a trifle out of hand."

"I thought those horrid men were making a lot of noise," said Mrs. Ukridge.

Ukridge preserved a gloomy silence. Of all the disasters of that stricken field, I think the one that came home most poignantly to him was the loss of the whisky. It seemed to strike him like a blow.

"Isn't it about time to collect these men and explain things?" I suggested. "I don't believe any of them know you've come back."

"They will!" said Ukridge grimly, coming out of his trance. "They soon will! Where's Beale! Beale!"

The Hired Retainer came running out at the sound of the well-remembered voice.

"Lumme, Mr. Ukridge, sir!" he gasped.

It was the first time Beale had ever betrayed any real emotion in my presence. To him, I suppose, the return of Ukridge was as sensational and astonishing an event as a re-appearance from the tomb. He was not accustomed to find those who had shot the moon revisiting their ancient haunts.

"Beale, go round the place and tell those scoundrels that I've come back, and would like a word with them on the lawn. And, if you find any of them stealing the fowls, knock them down!"

"I 'ave knocked down one or two," said Beale, with approval. "That Charlie—"

"Beale," said Ukridge, much moved, "you're an excellent fellow! One of the very best. I will pay you your back wages before I go to bed."

"These fellars, sir," said Beale, having expressed his gratification, "they've bin and scattered most of them birds already, sir. They've bin chasin' of them this half-hour back."

Ukridge groaned.

"Scoundrels! Demons!"

Beale went off.

"Millie, old girl," said Ukridge, adjusting the ginger-beer wire behind his ears and hoisting up his grey flannel-trousers, which showed an inclination to sag, "you'd better go indoors. I propose to speak pretty chattily to these blighters, and in the heat of the moment one or two expressions might occur to me which you would not like. It would hamper me, your being here."

Mrs. Ukridge went into the house, and the vanguard of the audience began to come on to the lawn. Several of them looked flushed and dishevelled. I have a suspicion that Beale had shaken sobriety into them. Charlie, I noticed, had a black eye.

They assembled on the lawn in the moonlight, and Ukridge, with his cap well over his eyes and his mackintosh hanging round him like a Roman toga, surveyed them sternly, and began his speech.

"You—you—you—you scoundrels! You blighters! You worms! You weeds!"

I always like to think of Stanley Featherstonehaugh Ukridge as I saw him at that moment. There have been times during a friendship of many years when his conduct did not recommend itself to me. It has sometimes happened that I have seen flaws in him. But on this occasion he was at his best. He was eloquent. He dominated his audience. Long before he had finished I was feeling relieved that he had thought of sending Mrs. Ukridge indoors when he did, and Beale was hanging on his words with a look in his eyes which I had never seen there before,—a look of reverence, almost of awe, the look of a disciple who listens to a master.

He poured scorn upon his hearers, and they quailed. He flung invective at them, and they wilted. Strange oaths, learned among strange men on cattle-ships or gleaned on the waterfronts of Buenos Ayres and San Francisco, slid into the stream of his speech. It was hard, he said in part, it was, upon his Sam, a little hard that a gentleman—a gentleman, moreover, who had done so much to stimulate local trade with large orders and what not—could not run up to London for five minutes on business without having his private grounds turned upside down by a gang of cattle-ship adjectived San Francisco substantives who behaved as if the whole of the Buenos Ayres phrased place belonged to them. He had intended to do well by them. He had meant to continue putting business in their way, expanding their trade. But would he after what had occurred? Not by a jugful! As soon as ever the sun had risen and another day begun, their miserable accounts should be paid in full, and their connection with him cut off. Afterwards it was probable that he would institute legal proceedings against them in the matter of trespass and wholesale damage to property, and if they didn't all end their infernal days in some dashed prison they might consider themselves uncommonly lucky, and if they didn't make themselves scarce in considerably under two ticks, he proposed to see what could be done with Beale's shot-gun. (Beale here withdrew with a pleased expression to fetch the weapon.) He was sick of them. They were blighters. Creatures that it would be fulsome flattery to describe as human beings. He would call them skunks, only he did not see what the skunks had done to be compared with them. And now they might go—*quick*!

We were quiet at the farm that night. Ukridge sat like Marius among the ruins of Carthage, and refused to speak. Eventually he took Bob with him and went for a walk.

Half an hour later I, too, wearied of the scene of desolation. My errant steps took me in the direction of the sea. As I approached, I was aware of a figure standing in the moonlight, gazing silently out over the waters. Beside the figure was a dog.

The dark moments of optimistic minds are sacred, and I would no more have ventured to break in on Ukridge's thoughts at that moment than, if I had been a general in the Grand Army, I would have opened conversation with Napoleon during the retreat from Moscow. I was withdrawing as softly as I could, when my foot grated on the shingle. Ukridge turned.

"Hullo, Garny."

"Hullo, old man." I murmured in a death-bedside voice.

He came towards me, Bob trotting at his heels: and, as he came, I saw with astonishment that his mien was calm, even cheerful. I should have known my Ukridge better than to be astonished. You cannot keep a good man down, and already Stanley Featherstonehaugh Ukridge was himself again. His eyes sparkled buoyantly behind their pince-nez.

"Garny, old horse, I've been thinking, laddie! I've got an idea! The idea of a lifetime. The best ever, 'pon my Sam! I'm going to start a duck farm!"

"A duck farm?"

"A duck farm, laddie! And run it without water. My theory is, you see, that ducks get thin by taking exercise and swimming about all over the place, so that, if you kept them always on land, they'd get jolly fat in about half the time—and no trouble and expense. See? What? Not a flaw in it, old horse! I've thought the whole thing out." He took my arm affectionately. "Now, listen. We'll say that the profits of the first year at a conservative estimate. . ."

THE END

A NOTE ABOUT THE AUTHOR

Sir Pelham Grenville Wodehouse (1881–1975) was an English author. Though he was named after his godfather, the author was not a fan of his name and more commonly went by P.G. Wodehouse. Known for his comedic work, Wodehouse created reoccurring characters that became a beloved staple of his literature. Though most of his work was set in London, Wodehouse also spent a fair amount of time in the United States. Much of his work was converted into "American" versions, and he wrote a series of Broadway musicals that helped lead to the development of the American musical. P.G. Wodehouse's eclectic and prolific canon of work both in Europe and America developed him to be one of the most widely read humorists of the 20th century.

A NOTE FROM THE PUBLISHER

Spanning many genres, from non-fiction essays to literature classics to children's books and lyric poetry, Mint Edition books showcase the master works of our time in a modern new package. The text is freshly typeset, is clean and easy to read, and features a new note about the author in each volume. Many books also include exclusive new introductory material. Every book boasts a striking new cover, which makes it as appropriate for collecting as it is for gift giving. Mint Edition books are only printed when a reader orders them, so natural resources are not wasted. We're proud that our books are never manufactured in excess and exist only in the exact quantity they need to be read and enjoyed.

bookfinity™

Discover more of your favorite classics with Bookfinity™.

- Track your reading with custom book lists.
- Get great book recommendations for your personalized Reader Type.
- Add reviews for your favorite books.
- AND MUCH MORE!

Visit **bookfinity.com** and take the fun Reader Type quiz to get started.

Enjoy our classic and modern companion pairings!

Classic & Modern

Printed in the USA
CPSIA information can be obtained
at www.ICGtesting.com
JSHW082352140824
68134JS00020B/2037

9 781513 270777